T0044179

Saka & Chorefuji Present

Once Upon a Witch's Death

THE TALE OF THE ONE THOUSAND TEARS OF JOY

"You're going to die, Meg."
My teacher said this to me suddenly.
My name is Meg Raspberry. I'm a witch in training.
"It'll happen in one year."
And apparently, I only have one year left to live

It all started with the declaration of my death.

"Behold, the power of a Sage."
She then tightly clenched her fist.
It happened in the blink of an eye.

Hundreds of thousands, millions of stars burned brightly, lighting up the night sky that moments ago was lit only by the full moon. The Milky Way appeared across the heavens, sparkling against a backdrop of interstellar clouds in a dazzling array of colors.
"A sight like this is probably only visible from the edge of the earth."

CONTENTS

Characters

Meg Raspberry

An apprentice witch living in the small English town of Lapis. Meg's teacher tells her that she only has a year left to live. She is a ball of positivity with a bit of a mouth on her.

Faust

Also known as the Eternal Witch, one of the world-famous Seven Sages. Meg's teacher and mother figure who raised her from when she was a little girl. Faust possesses an All-Seeing Eye she can use to see past, present, and future.

Inori

Also known as the Wise Witch, another of the Seven Sages. Inori hails from the Far East. She spends most of her time working with medical corporations to develop new medicines.

Sophie Hayter

Also known as the Witch of Blessings, Sophie is a genius and the newest and youngest member of the Seven Sages. She also has quite an appetite.

Fine Cavendish

Meg's best friend and one of the few people who understand her. Fine is a lovely young lady and doesn't have a single bad bone in her body.

THE TALE OF THE ONE THOUSAND TEARS OF JOY

Saka Illustration by **Chorefuji**

Translation by Richard Tobin

Yen On
150 West 30th Street, 19th Floor
New York, NY 10001

Visit us at yenpress.com • facebook.com/yenpress • twitter.com/yenpress • yenpress.tumblr.com • instagram.com/yenpress

First Yen On Edition: April 2024
Edited by Yen On Editorial: Leilah Labossiere
Designed by Yen Press Design: Andy Swist

Library of Congress Cataloging-in-Publication Data
Names: Saka (Light novel author), author. | Chorefuji, illustrator. | Tobin, Richard (Translator), translator.
Title: Once upon a witch's death : the tale of the one thousand tears of joy / Saka ; illustration by Chorefuji ; translation by Richard Tobin.
Other titles: Aru majo ga shinu made. English
Description: First Yen On edition. | New York : Yen On, 2024
Identifiers: LCCN 2023057034 | ISBN 9781975379988 (hardcover)
Subjects: CYAC: Fantasy. | Witches—Fiction. | Quests (Expeditions)—Fiction. | LCGFT: Fantasy fiction. | Witch fiction. | Light novels.
Classification: LCC PZ7.1.S24567 On 2024 | DDC [Fic]—dc23
LC record available at https://lccn.loc.gov/2023057034

ISBNs: 978-1-9753-7998-8 (hardcover)
978-1-9753-7999-5 (ebook)

10 9 8 7 6 5 4 3 2 1

LSC-C

Printed in the United States of America

Once Upon a Witch's Death

THE TALE OF THE ONE THOUSAND TEARS OF JOY

Saka

Illustration by **Chorefuji**

NEW YORK

Chapter 1:
A Witch with
One Year
Left to Live

It all started with the declaration of my death.
"You're going to die, Meg."
My teacher said this to me suddenly.

My name is Meg Raspberry. I'm a witch in training.
"It'll happen in one year."
And apparently, I only have one year left to live.

It was one o'clock in the afternoon, and things were quiet in the study of our manor. The sun was shining, and the clouds were floating gently through the sky. It was a nice early-autumn day that also happened to be my seventeenth birthday. I was so caught off guard by the sudden remark that I could only chuckle.
"What's that, Teacher? You don't usually make jokes."
"It isn't a joke. You're fated to die."
She said that without even batting an eye as she continued flipping through the document she was reading. The silence in the room accentuated the ticking of the wall clock and the chirping of the birds outside.
"You must be joking."
"You know I'm not one to make jokes."
"Uh, then were you leading up to some kind of surprise?"
"Have I ever surprised you with anything before?"
"Oh, I know! It's one of those prank shows! All right, where are the cameras—?"

"Do you honestly think I would ever participate in such a program?"

"No..."

My teacher spoke to me in her usual tone and gave me a stern look.

"As unfortunate as it may be, I only speak the truth. You are going to die, Meg Raspberry. And it will happen exactly one year from now."

I gulped. It really wasn't a *you're-gonna-die-Meg* kind of day.

So let me get this straight. I'm gonna die? In a year? Like, die *die? But why? Why?* Pourquoi*?*

The same question kept running on repeat in my mind.

"Just so you know, Teacher... Today *iiis* kinda my birthday."

"I know." My teacher nodded to me. "A birthday isn't enough to change the truth. You will die. And your death appears to be unavoidable."

"There's that word again... So why, exactly?"

"You're cursed."

"I'm *cursed*?"

My teacher's expression became serious as she gave me a solemn nod.

"You've always been cursed. It's a curse that becomes evident when the accursed has only a year left to live, and for you, this curse kicked in on your seventeenth birthday. It's called Death's Decree."

"Death's Decree...?"

It was the first time I'd ever heard of the curse.

"It's an ancient curse, one that modern witches know nothing of. Think of it as an illness you're born with. As soon as you turn eighteen, your internal clock will go haywire, and you will age at a rate one thousand times faster than a normal person. That's ten years in three days and a hundred years in one month. That's the longest anyone ever lasts after the curse takes its effect: a month."

"That's horrifying."

I said this out loud, but the meaning of my teacher's words hadn't really sunk in yet. She must've picked up on this, because she then said, "Meg, come here," and beckoned me over to her.

"What is it?"

"Be still for me."

My teacher extended her pointer finger and placed it lightly on my forehead.

"Let this person bear witness."

She chanted an incantation, and a video-like image flashed into my mind—it was a vision. What I saw was an old woman sitting alone on a bench. She was wobbly and weak, almost like she was barely alive at all. Like if she took a single step, her leg would pop off. But at the same time, there was a strange familiarity to her. The old woman suddenly grasped at her chest and began moaning in agony before keeling over where she sat. Froth bubbled out of her mouth as she lay motionless on the bench. I was shown a vision of some random old woman's final moments.

"What the heck was that all about...?"

I didn't really know what to say after being shown something so miserable, but I guess my teacher was expecting such a reaction from me, because she simply nodded.

"That was you, one year from now."

"You just showed me *me*?!"

"Correct, my child. That is what awaits you when your curse fulfills itself. You will grow old and decrepit to the point that you can barely move. And then perish. This is your future."

"Man..."

My teacher's tone was so serious. There really wasn't any way it could be a joke.

The elderly woman she showed me did look like me after all,

and the vision felt less like being shown a video than it did like something real I experienced. While I didn't want to admit it, it was clear the woman in the vision was in fact me.

"What can I do to break this curse…?"

"There is no way to break it. Not now, at least."

"Where is the person who cast this curse on me? Surely you know where they are? Let's catch them and make them tell us how to break this curse…"

"Like I said, you were born with it. Think of it as a chronic illness. You're sick."

"That's not something you're supposed to say to a girl who just turned seventeen, Teach."

"I will take care of you for the remaining year so that you can rest in peace."

Can you believe how cold this woman is? You'd think she'd show a little bit more love for her precious pupil after the ten-plus years we've been living together. Love… What even is love? What is peace? A good meal around a nice dinner table? Dinner… What were we gonna have for dinner today anyway? Come to think of it, I think that sale at the market was supposed to be today?

All sorts of thoughts ran through my mind as I stood in a bit of a stupor, but my teacher had the kindness to snap me out of it by saying, "Well now, *that* was a joke," before continuing. "It's not as if there's no way to save you."

"So you do make jokes. Just the unfunny kind… Well, please hurry up and tell me what to do…"

"It won't be easy. Both time-wise and task-wise."

My teacher took out a bottle as she said this. It was a small bottle with thick glass in the shape of a hexagon that fit snugly in the palm of her hand, like a perfume bottle. It must've been old, though, because the glass itself was foggy.

"That's a weird-looking bottle you have there. The trash bin is over there if you want me to throw it out for you…?"

"Don't be so quick to run your mouth. Although, yes, this is just an ordinary bottle. For now, at least."

"For now?"

My teacher then waved her hand over the bottle.

"Ingrain and capture this moment."

Now, this was a spell I knew. It was time magic. The bottle was enveloped in magic and began to give off a faint rainbow-colored aura. I could tell my teacher had poured some of her magic into the item.

"I have enchanted this bottle. From today, you are tasked with gathering shards of emotion inside of it."

"And what are shards of emotion, if you don't mind me asking?"

"They are what they sound like. Strong emotions felt by other people. You are to collect these."

"Strong emotions."

"There is something called a *seed of life*. From the emotions people feel—joy, anger, grief, and pleasure—a seed can be created. And you shall make your own."

"So how do I do that?"

"By using this bottle. I've cast a time magic spell on it, and a powerful spell that can't be broken, at that. This bottle can capture human emotions and turn them into crystal shards for you to collect inside of it. You will need to collect joy from many different people, or more specifically, the tears shed by those when they feel happiness… You will collect tears of joy."

"Tears of joy…"

"Yes. You will need them to create your seed of life, which can be used to make you immortal. Which means you'll be able to negate any time limit imposed on your life."

After she finished saying this, my teacher gave the bottle a small tap.

"This is the same method I used to become the Eternal Witch.

You will follow in my footsteps. Through the power of the seed, you will not age a day unless you *choose* to end its effect. You'll prevent your biological clock from going awry, nullifying the effect of your curse. You can live your life as much as you want, and when you feel the time has come, you have the ability to end the seed's effect on you."

"So I'm gonna be immortal?"

"For as long as you keep the spell active."

"Whoa..."

I hadn't seen that coming. Just this morning, I was a lowly witch in training, but I was about to become immortal. What this meant was that I would become the same as my teacher, a witch who lived eternally. *Talk about a sweet gig. Wow. Now, this is love. Seriously, though. What the heck even is love?*

"Heh, I guess you *do* love your pupil, don'cha, Teacher? So how many tears does it take to make one of them seeds?"

"You'll need tears from one thousand people."

It felt like time stopped when I heard her say this.

"...Come again?"

"You need one thousand shards to fill this bottle. Or roughly two hundred milliliters, in terms of volume. You'll have twelve months to collect tears from one thousand people who cry true tears of joy."

"Is that, uh...gonna be easy?"

"While it is common for people to cry when sad and in pain, tears of joy aren't so easily shed. It took me, for example, one hundred years to gather them. And that was using various magics to keep myself alive until I could."

"Can I actually do it in a year? All that..."

"As I said, it is no small task. Almost impossible, even. You'd have to be a witch capable of miracles to ever hope to accomplish it."

"So it all comes down to talent, then… Well, thanks for sharing such a crappy story."
"Meg, wait! Where are you going? Wait! Meg!"

I'm Meg Raspberry, witch in training. And evidently, I only have a year left to live.

○

My parents passed away when I was very little, or so I was told. I don't have many memories of either of them. I don't know why or how they died. All I know is that my teacher took me in after seeing me in an orphanage and feeling bad for me.

"Come. From today, we are family, Meg Raspberry."

Even now, I could remember the first words my teacher said to me that day. And for whatever reason, I found myself looking back on those words now.
After leaving the witch's manor, I ran to a nearby river and sat on the dirt embankment. This spot was about halfway through the Witch's Forest toward the nearby town. There were so many green trees around; it always calmed me down. Though it also happened to be a popular date spot, and things could get a bit awkward when there was a couple present. Luckily, I had it all to myself for the time being.
The lush green leaves let in the perfect amount of sunlight from the bright blue sky above, creating a beautiful, soft ambience. With it being early autumn, it was a cool day. The gentle breeze tickled my cheeks.
To think such a perfect day was supposed to be my seventeenth birthday…

I'm going to die. But what does death really mean? Ask anyone, and they'll say it's the state or concept of being dead. Where all life ends. Nirvana. The idea of it is so grand that it's difficult to make sense of it at all. Death is something that happens on television, not in real life.

Seventeen was young, and I was healthy. Even after seeing that frail version of myself keel over, there was still no way to really process it. That said, the shocking image was seared into my memory, and it didn't feel good.

If I really was going to die in a year, then what would I have to show for it? I spent my entire life studying magic and working away like an idiot. And all that hard work would go to waste. If that's the case, what was the point of the life I'd lived so far?

I still didn't get why I had to die in the first place or what this last year was supposed to mean to me. I just wanted to give up on life, but a part of me still thought this was all some kind of elaborate prank, which was what was holding me together.

I fell limply onto the embankment. Something soon peered into my face.

"*Squeak.*"

It was Carbuncle, a familiar my teacher had summoned. He looked half-fox, half-ferret, and his fur was a beautiful green color, like an emerald. Though he was an animal, there were times when his cleverness seemed to outclass that of a human.

Carbuncle sat and stared at my face before offering a few friendly licks. I guess it was his way of trying to cheer me up.

"What is it, you cute little fluff-button?"

While there was a regalness to Carbuncle, he was a spoiled little bugger. I picked him up and pulled him over to me, burying my face in his soft belly. His belly was warm, so I loved snuggling against him.

"Who's a good boy, who's a good boy, who's a good boy? Oh, bet that feels good, doesn't it? Heh-heh, ha-ha-ha-ha, hee-hee."

I was petting and fawning over Carbuncle as he let out little squeals of joy—and they most definitely were of joy. He wasn't trying to escape our snuggle or anything. That's for sure.

"Oh, you're that girl who works for Lady Faust."

An unknown voice addressed me, so I looked up and found a girl around five years old watching me. I didn't know her, but it wasn't uncommon for people to recognize me. My teacher, after all, was Lady Faust, the Eternal Witch. One of the best witches in the entire world. There were few people who *didn't* know the witch Faust, which meant that by extension, a good number of townsfolk knew I was her apprentice. It wasn't unusual for such people to strike up a conversation with me.

The young girl approached me. She seemed happy.

"What are you doing?"

"Oh, you know. Just enjoying the twilight sky. Takin' a short break from life."

"Wow. Your friend is cute."

"Isn't he, though? Wanna pet him?"

"Yeah!"

The little girl kept saying, "You're so cute," in a high-pitched voice while she petted Carbuncle. Carbuncle's eyelids were heavy; he seemed comfy.

That's not what you do when I pet you, though?

"Did you come here by yourself? This is pretty far from town," I said to the little girl, and she responded with an enthusiastic nod.

"Yup! I want to ask Lady Faust a favor!"

"Oh yeah?"

"I want her to give Mummy lots of flowers so she can sleep tight!"

"Uh, what?"

"My mummy used to live in the hospital, but she finally moved out. But now, she never wakes up, and my daddy said that she finally gets to sleep after working very hard for a long time, so I wanna give her some flowers that smell nice."

"Is that right...?"

It sounded to me like the little girl's mother had died after a long fight with some illness. This little girl must not have fully understood the situation, because she simply wanted to give her mum some flowers.

Oh, right. This little girl doesn't know what death is yet, I thought to myself, and somehow, I saw myself in her.

Flowers, huh...?

"How about this? Do you mind if *I* help you get some flowers for your mummy?"

"Really?"

"Sure." I smiled. "I'll help you with your favor."

○

The girl and I followed the path back to town together.

"Hey, I dunno your name," the little girl said, carrying Carbuncle in her arms. I shrugged and answered:

"You really ought to introduce yourself before asking people their names, ya know."

"My daddy told me not to tell people I don't know my name, though."

"Well, it seems we've hit a bit of an educational paradox..."

We eventually managed to exchange names after another minute of back-and-forth around the conundrum. Her name was Anna, and she was the daughter of a doctor who lived in the center of town.

"So your dad's a doctor..."

It made sense. Anna was well-behaved and well-spoken for her age; this much even I could tell. She must've come from a good family.

"So what kind of flowers would you like to get for your mum?"

"Hmm, I wanna get her favorite flowers!"

"And those are…?"

"Pretty pink ones! Mummy said she saw them before! That there were lots of them, and they were super pretty! She always said she wanted to see them one more time."

"Uh, that's pretty vague. There are lots of flowers that are pink… Did she ever say their name?"

"Nope."

"So you wanted to ask Lady Faust for flowers you don't know about?"

"I figured she would know."

"Why would she…? Er, actually…I wouldn't put it past her to know exactly the right flower…"

That old hag… My beloved teacher would probably use her All-Seeing Eye to look into the past. While it was difficult to tell the future due to all the undecided variables, it was pretty easy for her to see the past, as everything was already set in stone. Needless to say, I wasn't capable of doing that. No one else was…

"I'm sorry, Anna. I'm not as good as my teacher yet, so I can't figure out the flower's name with no clues to go on like she can."

"Really? Well, it's okay. You don't have to feel so sad."

"Yeah… Thanks…"

Something about this hit me where it hurt, but I wasn't one to let myself get hung up on things.

"So she saw the flowers once before… Do you think your dad knows about the flowers?"

"I dunno, but my daddy is probably home right now! Wanna go see?"

"Yeah, let's go."

I thought maybe Anna's dad could offer a clue, so we decided to head for her house.

* * *

We continued along the riverside road, and the town gradually appeared on the horizon. This town was called Lapis, and it was a tranquil settlement in England with a population of about a hundred thousand people. Lapis was a long way from the bustling heart of London and was characterized by old brick buildings. It was what some might call a commuter town.

There was a railroad that connected the town to the capital, as well as the beginnings of what would become a subway that was still under construction. At the center of town was the square, from which extended four roads that led to the marketplace and residential areas. There was also an old clock tower that chimed in the evenings.

The marketplace was always bustling with people during the day, and there was a big park in the northern part of town. Lapis was an old town with a long history, and its people lived in harmony with the nature that surrounded it.

A part of that nature was the Witch's Forest, which was where my teacher and I lived in our manor far away from the town. There were many witches who lived in the larger cities throughout England, but my teacher and I were all Lapis had.

"If it ain't the disciple. Are ye runnin' errands fer Lady Faust today?"

"Heh-heh, I guess you could say that."

"You're that girl who works under Lady Faust. You here for work?"

"Sure am…"

"Oh? If it isn't Lady Faust's youngin'. Funny seeing you here this time of day. Would you like some chips?"

"Yes, thank you, Granny. Do you have enough for my friend, too?"

"I sure do."

* * *

Lapis was full of friendly people. They accepted me for who I was, even though I was a witch. We were sharing the chips as we continued down the road, when I realized Anna was staring at me while she petted Carbuncle.

"What's up?"

"You're famous."

"Well, yeah. I am the disciple of one of the Seven Sages, Lady Faust, after all."

"Seven Say-jez?"

"Think of them as the world's seven smartest mages."

In this world, there were witches and wizards called mages who could harness special power beyond human intelligence. Of all the mages in the world, the Seven Sages were recognized by the Council of Magic—an international association that oversaw the use of magic—as highly skilled in their witchcraft or wizardry.

My teacher, the Eternal Witch, Faust, was one of the Seven Sages and a powerful witch who embodied the teachings of ancient witchcraft. For as long as magic had existed, witches had used their power to help people, and people had repaid them with gifts of thanks. To this day, my teacher still maintained this relationship with the people. This was why the townspeople were so fond of her, and that made me the beloved disciple of a powerful witch.

"So are you gonna be like Lady Faust someday?"

"Yeah, I sure—" Doubts flooded my mind.

—will...or I wanted to. If I weren't destined to die, maybe I could've been like her someday. A great witch, loved by all. I mean, that's been my goal up until now. What I've strived so hard for, in my own way. But if all my striving is going to take me to a lonely death as an old lady, then what's it all for? Isn't that a bit too cruel? So all my effort was all for naught? Why me?

"To heck with it!"

"Ack! You scared me!"

"That's enough doom and gloom, Anna. Let's get a move on!"

"Did I say something gloomy?"

"No, not really! But that's neither here nor there!"

"You're kind of weird."

"I was born this way!"

I'd never been good at thinking about complicated things and minutiae. Some people have gone as far as saying that positivity was my main personality trait.

Anna's house was located in the center of town. It doubled as her father's practice, as they had a doctor's office built into the house.

"This is my home!"

"That's one big home you've got there."

It was a three-story house made of bricks, which at a glance looked like a regular old home, despite the built-in office. As it was clearly larger than any of the surrounding houses, it was easy to imagine that Anna's family was on the wealthier side.

"Is there something wrong?"

"Hmm? Oh, no. I just remember coming here before. But wow, Anna. I'm jealous."

"Of what?"

"I mean, look at your house. It's beautiful. You guys must be loaded. You should see our house. It's a shabby old manor."

"Do you want money?"

"Yup. You gonna give me some?"

"Ha-ha. No."

"Dang it."

We exchanged shameless banter as we entered the home. As soon as we stepped through the door, Anna called out, "Daddy, we have a guest," before running down the hall into another room. I trailed slowly behind her. She let go of Carbuncle as soon as we were inside, and he came to my feet. I bent down and extended a hand so he could climb onto my shoulder, which was when I noticed the dust collecting at the creases where the wall met the floor.

I looked around, and there was dust and other small blotches of dirt and stains here and there around the house. It was clear that it was being cleaned, but not enough for the more intricate spots to be spotless; whoever was doing the cleaning wasn't used to it.

"You think a doctor would be more concerned about germs, am I right?"

"Squeak."

A short walk down the hallway brought me to a door with light peeking through the cracks. It looked like the living quarters and doctor's office were connected from the inside. I poked my head through the doorway and found Anna with a man who was presumably her father.

"Anna, I told you not to come in here without asking first."

"Daddy! We have a guest!"

"A guest? Are they feeling ill?"

"Nope, I'm as healthy as a horse."

I couldn't help butting in, and my eyes met his. He was a gentle-looking man with short blond hair and glasses. As soon as we saw each other, we both said, "Ah."

"Oh, it's Dr. Hendy."

"And you're Lady Faust's..."

"It's Meg. Meg Raspberry."

"Ah yes. Meg."

"Do you know my daddy, Miss Meg?"

Anna looked a bit confused. I nodded to her.

"Know him? He's one of our best customers. Come to think of it, I've been here a few times before."

"Really?"

"Really. Your dad buys medicine from us, and I deliver it. I knew this house looked familiar."

"That makes sense, seeing as you always make your deliveries on the doctor's office side. You never met Anna before?"

"Nope. This was our first meeting."

Medicine used to be made by witches. The witches made the medicine, and the doctors used it to heal people. This symbiotic relationship continued throughout history. But in modern times, businesses took over producing medicine, and the number of witches who made it decreased significantly. Instead, witches went on television, became scholars, and were treated more like celebrities. How witches were perceived and how they used their magic had changed over the years.

Most witches nowadays didn't usually go out of their way to make or use medicines from herbs even for themselves, but these herb-based medicines were able to enhance the effects of medicine provided by doctors when used in tandem. That being said, there were people who found medicine enhanced with magic a bit off-putting, so most doctors strayed away from prescribing it. Dr. Hendy was one of the few good doctors who still used a combination of both medicines. He knew the medicinal value of witch medicine.

Dr. Hendy cocked his head slightly in confusion and asked his daughter, "So why did you bring little Miss Meg here?"

Anna happily hopped up as she answered his question.

"Miss Meg is gonna give Mummy flowers!"

"Flowers?"

"Anna came to visit Lady Faust to ask for flowers for her mother's grave to help her sleep better."

I whispered this into the doctor's ear, and he whispered back, "Is that right?" His expression was gentle and also sad as he said this.

"Do you happen to know what kind of flowers your wife liked?"

"Flowers, huh…? She used to decorate the house with them, but I'm not sure what kind she liked."

"Hrm… I thought maybe you could give us a hint."

Dr. Hendy realized my bewilderment, and then he clapped his hands together and said, "Oh, right. We do have some photo albums. Perhaps they will offer a clue. You can find them in the study."

"I'll go check!"

"Whoa, wait up, Anna. I'll go with you…"

The quick footsteps of Anna's little feet could be heard pitter-pattering out of the room before I could even react. My eyes met with the doctor's, and we shared a smile.

"Your daughter's a little ball of energy."

"She really is. My wife was bedridden due to her sickness, but her daughter has grown up quite healthy. Her mum must be happy in heaven."

"Did she pass away recently?"

"It hasn't even been a week yet… I'm sorry, I intended on going to visit Lady Faust about it, but we ended up having the funeral with just our immediate families."

"It's fine, really. I'm sure things have been tough for you."

The air in the room grew solemn. I never liked this feeling.

"I'm sorry for intruding on you during work like this, by the way."

"Oh, no. It's fine, really. I just finished my morning examinations. You're welcome to join me for a cup of tea, if you wish."

"I'd love to."

○

I followed Dr. Hendy to the kitchen. On our way there, I caught a glimpse of his bathroom. There were still three toothbrushes on the sink. One child-sized and two for adults. I recognized the same pattern when we entered the kitchen, with mugs and plates all in sets of three. Signs of Anna's mother were still all over the house.

Oh. Time has stopped for this house.

"I still haven't had time to clean up yet. There's a lot that's been left as is."

Dr. Hendy said this with a bit of a wry smile as he heated up the teakettle.

"I know I should probably start cleaning up her things."

He seemed so drained, like he was slowly fading away where he stood. Even though we were having a chat, it felt more like he was talking to himself than me.

"Is there anything I can help you with?"

"No, I wouldn't want to bother a guest. Please make yourself comfortable."

If that was what the owner of the house wanted, I could only oblige. I sat down on his sofa and gave the room a quick scan. The first thing I noticed was a shelf full of bottled-up herbs. It was quite rare to see someone collect medicinal herbs in such a way.

"The herbs catch your eye?"

"I was just surprised at how many you have… A lot of those are pretty rare."

"Lady Faust used to complain about how difficult some herbs are to acquire. I had a friend who's knowledgeable about medicinal herbs start sending these to me."

"So that's why you sometimes bring us herbs to use."

It must've taken a lot of effort to learn about and collect such medicinal herbs. Hats off to you, doctor.

"Are those herbs for medicinal use as well?"

There was a second shelf with a few bottles of different herbs on it. The bottles were filled with chopped-up dried leaves and stems.

"Oh, those were herbs my wife used to collect. I'm not sure what she intended to use them for…"

Dr. Hendy opened a cabinet as he said this and moved things around.

"What are you doing?"

"Oh, I'm just looking for the tea. I haven't had a chance to drink any ever since my wife passed."

"You should get on top of that. I'll have you know that most men know their way around the house these days."

"Ha-ha, that hurts to hear."

"I think this may be what you're looking for."

I got up from the sofa and picked up one of the bottles full of herbs.

"Are you sure that's tea?"

"Sure, it's herbal tea. I'm pretty sure that's what these were meant for. There are lots of benefits to drinking it, you know, and it tastes great, too. I know my tea well, so you can leave it to me."

I examined the shelf full of herbs. One in particular caught my eye. I picked it up and held it in my hand.

"Oh wow…"

Well, this is a surprise, I thought to myself. It was a rare herb. I figured we may as well try it, seeing as it was there and all.

I spread out a paper towel on the table and picked out a mix of herbs to place onto it. Then I concentrated on my inner flow of magic before holding my hand over the mixture and chanting a twelve-part incantation.

"Grass and trees—heed my commands—show us—your inner power.

I ask you—come to us—in your truest form—as sustenance.

A part of us you shall become—together with us always—and one—we shall be."

The space around us darkened, and the collection of herbs

glowed faintly. It was a magical reaction. Small wisps of smoke rose from the leaves, and the herbs' aroma filled the room.

"Wowee!"

Evidently, Anna had returned to the room at some point and was watching with wide eyes as I worked my magic.

"Is this magic?"

"It sure is. Pretty neat, eh?"

"Yeah!"

"It really is curious, isn't it?"

Dr. Hendy was nodding, watching with great interest as well.

"What did you just do, Miss Meg?"

"I just roasted the leaves a bit. It'll help bring out the flavor."

"Can you do anything you want?"

"Not *anything*. It takes a lot of knowledge to cast a spell."

Magic was often misconstrued as miracles with no limits, but that wasn't the case. There were many fields of magic, and to create the intended effects required significant knowledge of the substances and phenomenology at hand.

To ignite a fire required magical friction against a combustible substance. To create water required breaking apart and merging its elements. Whether something exploded or burned depended on the method used.

A mage needed to understand the principles of physics, then fill the gaps with magic, which required knowledge. This left most mages with very narrow fields of expertise. I was studying pharmacy and botany, but there were those who studied different subjects such as science or chemistry.

The point is, you need to know your stuff if you want to be a mage.

Time magic, or chronomancy, that my teacher used was on a whole 'nother level of its own in terms of difficulty. The theory of time had components of both physics and philosophy, and to pull off time magic required a thorough knowledge of pretty much everything.

Plus, my teacher could use her All-Seeing Eye. My best guess was that it took an immense amount of knowledge to manifest a time magic spell itself, and then she needed knowledge of the human body and medicine on top of it to actually use it on a person. It wasn't something I could ever hope to pull off.

"So did you find the album?"

"Yeah, I did! Here it is."

Anna placed the album on top of the desk. It was very thick, with a somewhat dated cover. The album was clearly filled with memories spanning many years. We opened it up, and every page was packed with pictures.

There were pictures of Dr. Hendy with a beautiful woman. This must've been Anna's mother. She had sharp features, but there was something vaguely ephemeral about her.

The album started with pictures of Dr. Hendy and his wife. Then, somewhere along the line, Anna joined them. The family's entire history, every step they'd taken together, was all kept safe in this album.

"There sure are a lot of pictures from trips in here..."

"My wife and I loved to travel. We traveled the world together before Anna was born."

"How extravagant. I'd like to travel the world, too."

"I understand Lady Faust travels quite often, does she not?"

"For work—and she always leaves me home. I would only get in the way if I went along."

"Well, someday, when you're a full-fledged witch, I'm sure Lady Faust will want to bring you along."

"Someday...?"

I don't have a someday. I almost said this out loud, but I swallowed my words. I flipped through some pages to try and change the subject.

Dr. Hendy and his wife really had traveled all over the world. America, Germany, France, Russia, and Asia. They'd traversed the globe.

As I flipped through the pages, I could hear Dr. Hendy remarking here and there, "I remember that day."

"Here's a picture from when we were in Asia."

"Those are Japanese clothes and buildings, right? They look so old and traditional."

"Japan is a country of tradition. It was one of my wife's favorite places we visited. She always said she wanted to take Anna to see it."

"Wow, I didn't know it was such a nice country."

"They have a unique food culture as well. Lots of fish and fried foods, unlike what we have here. It all felt so new. But what left the biggest impression on us was a strange experience we shared there."

"A strange experience?" I asked with a puzzled tone, and Dr. Hendy continued with a nod.

"We went to visit a temple on the mountainside, and it was snowing. The thing is, it was the middle of spring and warm outside. Strange, isn't it?"

"So it was snowing during the spring?"

"Yes, and it was as bright and sunny a day as there ever has been. There wasn't the slightest sign of snow in the sky, and yet it snowed. And the snow was pink... It was very beautiful. My wife and I could've watched it all day. It's something that's stayed with me after all these years."

"Pink snow during the spring, eh...? You don't say..."

I looked through the album for a picture of the event but couldn't find any.

"Looking back, there's so much I couldn't do for her…"

Dr. Hendy muttered this to himself quietly.

"Just before she had Anna, she said she wanted to take our daughter to Japan when spring came around. But once Anna was born, my wife did everything around the house. I focused on my job instead, thinking I needed to feed my family. I worked and worked and worked. If I knew things would turn out this way, I would've figured out a way to make the trip."

This is something that must be eating away at Dr. Hendy. The fact that he couldn't do anything for his deceased wife. That he couldn't save her, even though he's a doctor. There must be a long list of little things like this accumulating inside him.

He was hunched over, making his frame appear small, and smiling weakly.

I turned the pages until Anna started appearing in pictures. Compared to the beginning of the album, which was filled with pictures taken in foreign lands, the pictures of Anna were all taken in England. The pictures were of the house, of the park in Lapis, and of family gatherings. And the final pages were all taken in the hospital, of Anna and her mother smiling. Her mother was very thin.

"When did your wife get sick?"

"It happened about a year ago. That's when she grew severely ill and was hospitalized."

"A whole year…"

It was the same amount of time I had left to live. I wondered at which point Anna's mother had finally accepted her death. She didn't seem too distraught in any of the pictures, at least. In fact, I'd never seen such a happy person before. Her mother had a big smile in every picture in the album. She must've been truly happy.

Looking through the album, I knew I wouldn't smile like her were I to die as I was now.

As I continued to flip through the pages, it struck me that almost every picture had flowers in it. Roses, cornflower, irises, lilies, chamomile, hibiscus, peonies, jasmine, hibiscus—the list went on of flowers that decorated her hospital bed.

"Was it your wife who bought these flowers?" I asked Dr. Hendy, and he replied with a nod.

"That's right. She used to buy them at flower shops or would tag along when I went to buy herbs. She was always trying something new with them, decorating them in different ways."

"Mummy always bought the prettiest flowers."

"Wow… That's really impressive…"

But it didn't help. I had no idea what kind of flowers Anna's mother would've wanted. The more I thought about it, the more bewildered I became.

"Argh! Now I'm just confused!"

I began scratching my head—a habit of mine when I dealt with stress—and Dr. Hendy chuckled wryly.

"Maybe we should take a break. Let's enjoy the tea you so kindly prepared for us."

"Oh, I almost forgot about that…"

We reheated the water and placed the freshly roasted tea leaves in the kettle, steeping them for a few minutes before pouring three cups of tea. The moment the tea left the kettle, its rich aroma expanded throughout the kitchen.

"Oh wow! That smells sooo good!"

Anna looked at me with wide eyes that twinkled with happiness, and I smirked back at her.

"Right? Herbal tea is the best. I actually added a secret ingredient this time, too."

"A secret ingredient?"

The sensation of the delicious tea filled my mouth and brought with it the smell of flowers. Then it hit me.

Pink snow, on a spring day, during warm weather, at the foot of a mountain.

If the flowers Anna's mother used to decorate the house were for her husband and daughter, then *that* was the only flower worth giving back to her.

"Hey, Anna. Is your mum sleeping in a spot near here?"

"Uh-huh. It's close by."

"I'd like you to take me there."

I smiled.

"I'll show you the pink snow and the flowers your mum wanted to see again."

○

It was a five-minute walk to the graveyard where Anna's mother was buried.

"That's one nice grave. Is this where your mum is sleeping?"

"Mm-hmm."

I touched the gravestone, and Carbuncle, who was at my feet, nudged me with his nose curiously. There was something both lifeless and warm at the same time about the letters carved into the stone.

Beneath this spot lay *death*.

"I already know, really."

"Hmm? Know what?"

"That Mummy isn't ever gonna wake up again."

Anna's expression didn't change in the slightest as she quietly murmured this. Her eyes were looking straight ahead, staring at something far away. It felt like she was holding back sadness that was trying to flow out.

"Oh, so you knew..."

She knew her mother was dead and that they would never meet

again. That she wasn't coming back. Anna knew everything but held it all in. Maybe she didn't know exactly what death was, but she could tell what it meant.

"Hey, Miss Meg."

"What's up?"

"Do you think the world's greatest witch could…maybe wake Mummy up?"

Bringing someone back to life—throughout magic's long history, there were many mages who had devoted their lives to making this a possibility, but not one had succeeded.

It's something my teacher had told me many times before: It's arrogant to try to bring someone back to life. Magic is to know the flow of life and listen to the voice of reason. Therefore, we need to accept what we see before us, and must do what we can with what we have.

"No, there isn't a mage who can wake your mother up."

I didn't know how to answer Anna, but I didn't want to lie to her, nor did it feel like I should. I kept my eyes locked with hers and slowly continued.

"God has a plan for this world. It's a plan that we can't disobey. We call this *fate*."

"You're fated to die, Meg. It'll happen in one year."

"It was your mother's fate to go to sleep when she did."

I was telling this little girl the same thing my teacher had told me only a short while earlier. Ironically enough, by being the one having to say these things, I was slowly beginning to comprehend my own death.

"Would it be bad if I asked God to wake my mummy up?"

"Have you ever heard of a thing called a zombie?"

"Yeah."

"Do you know why they attack people?"

"No. Why?"

"Because someone woke them up from a deep sleep against their will. They're actually just mad."

"So Mummy would get mad if we woke her up?"

"Oh yeah, *super mad*. That's why everyone is too afraid to wake them up. Even God."

"Mummy's too sleepy."

"Well, just think of how hard she worked. She must be tired, so let her rest. That's all people really want to do anyway."

"People…"

"So, Anna. Even if we make flowers bloom for your mum, it won't wake her up. Do you still want to make them bloom?"

"Yeah."

"Why's that?"

"Because I think it'd make my mummy happy."

Anna looked straight into my eyes as she said this.

"Before she went to sleep, she told me…"

"Told you what?"

"To take care of Daddy."

My heart ached when I heard her say this.

"Daddy's been really sad. He always looks at pictures of Mummy with a sad look on his face. So I think he'd be happy knowing Mummy was sleeping well."

"Do you actually want to get these flowers for your dad?"

I asked Anna this, and she nodded coyly.

"I want Mummy to sleep tight and Daddy to feel better."

Is that what's going on here? This girl wanted to fulfill her promise to her mother and kept it all to herself. I'm sure she never thought she'd suddenly lose someone so important to her like this. Her mother is gone. And her father's depressed. Anna came looking for Lady Faust knowing she had to do something but not what to do.

I'd thought she was just some kid who innocently came to ask the witches for some flowers for her mother at first. But I was wrong. She's trying to accept her mother's death and support her mourning father. It's not just about Dr. Hendy, either. It's Anna, too. They both have big gaping holes in their hearts left behind by the mother and wife they lost too soon.

Even though she was sad and lonely like her father, she was trying to do something about it. For her family.

I was moved by Anna's strength. I could feel it in my heart. I realized that Anna knew far more about death than me. I could barely process mine.

"There you are."

I turned around when I heard a voice call out suddenly from behind us and saw Dr. Hendy waving as he approached.

"I'm glad I caught up to you."

Dr. Hendy must've jogged here, because he spoke between harsh pants.

"Why did you come as well, Dr. Hendy?"

"I couldn't get my mind off what you were going to do, so I closed the practice for an extra hour before the afternoon check-ups."

"What?! Think of the patients, Doc!"

My words elicited a grin from Dr. Hendy, though he seemed at a loss for how to respond.

This just won't do. What a bad father. I guess it's my job to give him the push he needs.

It occurred to me that maybe I was the one who could make time start again for these two. These two had taught me what it meant to lose someone important…to lose a family member.

I figured this would be the only way to fill the hole in their hearts.

"So, Meg. Have you figured out which flowers were my wife's favorite?"

"I think so, though there's no way to really prove it."

I placed my hand softly on the gravestone.

"Dr. Hendy. I think the reason your wife used to decorate the house with those flowers was to show Anna the same precious sights she saw when she traveled the world with you."

"Precious sights, you say?"

"Yes, they were precious to her because she shared them with you on those trips."

I looked at each of them with a gentle gaze.

"All the flowers Anna's mother used for decorations were national flowers."

Roses were for America.

Cornflowers for Germany.

Irises for France.

All the flowers Anna's mother used to decorate their house with were the national flowers of the countries she and her husband had visited before Anna was born.

"I think that, by showing Anna the different flowers she loved from countries around the world, she thought she could show Anna the world, like she'd seen it."

"Really, now...?"

"But there was one flower she could never decorate the house with. And I think *that's* the exact flower she wanted to show Anna so badly."

I crouched down to Anna's level and looked her straight in the eyes.

"Anna. There's a plant in the Far East called the Yoshino cherry tree."

"Yoh-sheeno?"

"Yoshino cherry blossoms, better known as sakura flowers, bloom in the spring."

In Dr. Hendy's herb cabinet, I'd discovered the pink snow that fell at the beginning of spring, which was how I figured out what the snow really was. He had a small herb bottle of sakura petals. Normally, these were used for tea, but I had a different purpose in mind.

"Hear my call—"

I cupped my hands around a small handful of the petals and chanted a twelve-part spell.

"O abundant earth—vast and bountiful—I ask for a miracle—conjure a vibrant spring once found on your sacred ground."

The surrounding light gathered around my hand, causing the immediate area around us to become as dark as night. The light enveloping my hand created a firefly-like glow that shone through the darkness. This was magic.

"Let illusions rise—a dream that takes a form—the hope this dream imparts us—a beacon in the storm—reveal the hues of the distant East—and upon your beauty—"

I continued my spell, and the petals resting in the palm of my hand turned vibrant and fresh, like they'd been when they were just picked. I didn't have a sakura sapling or seed, but I didn't need one. I could work with the grass and trees around me to construct fake sakura trees. It was all thanks to the bottle of sakura petals and herbs.

I turned the green of leaves into the vibrant pink color of the sakura petals, and in the blink of an eye, the leaves soon transformed into flowers. A bright light shone as everything around us turned a brilliant shade of pink.

This was a miracle, a scientifically impossible occurrence. It was created by filling the gaps of various phenomena with mystic power—the miracle of magic.

My power merged the nature around us to change it into something new.

"—let our eyes feast."

This last verse triggered the final transformation.

"Whoa..."

Dr. Hendy and Anna looked up at the leaves in awe, and Carbuncle zoomed around in excitement.

Sakura trees sprang up all around us.

Pink snow. That's exactly how it appeared as the flower petals simultaneously began fluttering to the ground.

"Wow..."

"This is replication magic. I used it to make sakura trees, but it is more of a momentary illusion than an actual transformation."

I wiped my nose as I bragged, but honestly, I think I was more surprised than they were. My magic had affected a much larger radius than I'd initially intended. There were a hundred trees spreading in every direction.

The sight would likely last a few hours before the plants reverted to their original forms, but its beauty truly was miraculous.

Maybe this really is a miracle. I even found myself toying with such a thought.

Dr. Hendy watched the flower petals in awe before eventually snapping out of his stupor and muttering the words "I remember this.

"It was so long ago. Long before Anna was born, when we went to the East. Remember how I recalled there being pink snow, even though it was spring? It was Iris who said this. We watched

the pink flower petals cover the earth, and she commented how it reminded her of snow. That comment must've sat with me, because I'd remembered it as actual snow all this time."

"I'm sure your wife wanted to take Anna to Asia to show her this very sight. For your wife, this was a special memory she shared with you and something she thought should never be forgotten. Since getting actual sakura trees wasn't feasible, she probably got these petals for you instead."

"Is that right…?"

"That's not all, either. Did you know all those herbs in your kitchen were picked out especially for you? Every bottle on that shelf heals something that you deal with."

Rosemary, lavender, hibiscus, chamomile, ginger. These herbs calmed the nerves, relieved stress, and warmed up the body. Most of the herbs in Dr. Hendy's wife's cabinet had some sort of relaxing effect.

Being a doctor was a stressful job, both mentally and physically. I could tell Dr. Hendy's wife left behind the perfect herb cabinet for him.

"You still might have regrets about neglecting your wife for your work while she was alive, but I think your wife knew how you truly felt. Look at all the herbs, the sakura petals, and the flowers she used to get for you… There aren't many people who show their love for their family as she did. I think she truly loved you and your daughter from the bottom of her heart."

"Meg…"

I gently tightened my grip around Anna's hand as she looked up at the falling sakura petals.

"I think your mother is fine now. She finally got to show her beloved daughter the sight she wanted to most. You don't have to worry anymore."

Then it happened. Anna's big wide eyes went glossy.

"I don't need…to hold it in anymore?"

"Nope. Everything is all right now."

"Really?"

"Really. You did good, Anna."

When she heard these words, two big tears escaped Anna's watery eyes and ran down either side of her cheeks.

"Ever since Mummy went away…I've been so lonely…and Daddy is always so sad…and Mummy's gone…forever and ever…"

"Anna…!"

Dr. Hendy gave his daughter a firm hug.

"I'm so sorry, Anna. Daddy feels better now. I won't let you feel lonely ever again. Okay?"

"Okay…!"

Large tears gushed out and ran down the sides of both of their faces. It was like the feelings they had both been holding deep inside were being let out all at once.

Watching them made me think of something: Anna's mother was smiling in every picture there was of her, even up until her death. I'm sure this wasn't because she was unafraid of her own death, but that when her family looked back on their time with her, she wanted their memories to be good. She wanted them to remember her smiling. She wanted to be a wonderful memory.

"I think your mother wanted you to smile after she passed away…"

Tears fell from their cheeks like the pink petals from the trees above, and I heard the soft tinkling of crystallized shards falling into the bottle at my waist.

"Thank you, Miss Meg."

By the time my magic's effect wore off, the sun was low in the sky, and our shadows extended long on the ground.

I walked the pair back to their home, where we said our good-byes.

"Do you think that was enough for your mum?"

"Yeah, I think she's super happy."

"Even though they weren't real sakura trees?"

"Well...um...yeah..."

You gotta give me something to work with, kid, I privately lamented to myself, when Dr. Hendy came forward with a bow of his head.

"It looks like my daughter and I hadn't moved on since my wife passed. But you made me realize that's not what Iris would've wanted. She wanted us to be happy more than anything else. I don't think I could've figured this out without you."

"You need to be the father Anna needs, and I have faith you can be. Although, is your practice okay? You ended up staying out during your afternoon check-ups."

"Ha-ha... I think my patients will forgive me for one day."

Just as Dr. Hendy said this, the clock at the center of town rang out, indicating that it was five o'clock.

"Oh man! I gotta run, or Teach is gonna kill me! Until we meet again...!"

I spun on my heel and prepared to sprint, but then Anna called out, "Miss Meg!"

I turned once more to see her staring at me with sparkles in her eyes.

"Are you gonna be like Lady Faust someday, too?"

"Huh? What's this all of a sudden?"

"I think you will! You showed us my mummy's favorite flowers! I think you'll be a great witch, just like Lady Faust! I really do! So promise me you will become one!"

"Uhhh... 'Kay..."

I couldn't say it. That I only had a year left to live.

My inability to come up with a response must've been all too clear, because Dr. Hendy picked up his daughter from behind and stepped in.

"You don't have to worry about young Meg, Anna. She will become one of the greatest mages to ever live."

He was being so straightforward; I could tell there wasn't a doubt in the doctor's mind when he said that. In fact, his eyes were beginning to sparkle just like his daughter's. I wiped my nose to hide my embarrassment.

"Fine! When I become a real witch, I'll fulfill our promise by showing you a real sakura tree."

"Really?!"

I couldn't help smiling at the glimmer in Anna's eyes, and I nodded firmly.

"Yup! You just wait and see!"

○

The evening view of this town was one thing I really liked about it.

There were people on their way home from work, the market was alive with busybody housewives, and the smell of stew for dinner escaped from the brick homes into the streets.

It was a nice sight to see but also somewhat lonely. I felt something warm brush up against my leg as I walked. It was Carbuncle, and he was scratching at my feet.

"Oh, whoops. I completely forgot about you."

I picked him up, and he yowled at me. Evidently, he was mad.

"C'mere, you," I said and gave him a good petting, which he seemed to like because before long, he responded with his usual "*Squeak...*" and then quieted down.

The squeak means he's happy. I'm sure of it...

I placed him on my shoulder, then continued down the same path we'd used to enter the town.

"Hey! You're Lady Faust's disciple! You on your way home?"

"Yup."

"It's the disciple. Hope you had a good day."
"You too."
"Wait! Would you mind bringing this to Lady Faust for me? It's a little treat for dinner."
"Thanks, Granny."

I was always greeted by many people when I walked these streets. Their smiles stayed with me that day, though. I then recalled a day long ago when I'd walked this same road with my teacher.

I used to be bullied by the kids in town when I was younger. We would get into fights, and if I fought back, they would beat me down with their numbers. That day, I'd been clenching my fists in frustration as I sat in a corner of the town.
"There you are, Meg."
It was my teacher. She'd come to pick me up.
"I don't know why you always get into fights."
"It's 'cause the other kids call me the 'evil witch's' underling!"
I was biting my lip.
"Even though you're the bestest witch ever…"
"I see, so you are angry on my behalf."
I nodded, and my teacher looked happy as she reached down and grabbed my hand.
"Let us buy some bread, my child."
She said this, then slowed her walking pace to match my own.
"Hey, Teacher? Do you think it'd be better if I wasn't here?"
"Why would you think that?"
"Well, everyone always says bad things about you because I'm here…"
I was looking down when I said this, but I felt my teacher's

hands cradle both sides of my cheeks and pull my head up. I could see myself in her big eyes.

"Listen to me, Meg. If you think what you did was right, then there is no reason for you to look down. You should be proud of yourself."

"I should?"

"Yes. If you have pride, you can make it through anything. Even if it feels like the entire world is against you, you should always do what you feel is right. You have the courage and strength to fight for those important to you when you feel they've been harmed. All you need is pride, and you will be invincible."

My teacher looked straight into my eyes, and her usual bold grin made its way across her face.

"Be proud, Meg. Your pride in yourself makes me proud as well."

After that, my teacher bought us some freshly baked bread. It had felt warm in my hands, and its fresh smell had filled the evening air around us. I could still remember forgetting all about the fight, and my younger self just wished the moment could last forever.

"Look up at the sky, Meg. It's the first star of the night. Isn't it brilliant?"

"Yeah…"

My teacher's words had made it feel like I'd received permission to be there—to live. That's what it felt like to me when I was younger, at least.

I'm sure she and I looked a lot like Dr. Hendy and his daughter did that day.

My teacher had told me about my impending death. But somehow, I knew she wasn't declaring my death. There was always meaning to whatever my teacher did. At the very least, she wouldn't give me a problem I truly couldn't solve. That much I was sure of.

"She wanted me to become a great mage someday, eh…?"

I looked up, and the sky was slowly shifting to night, and just like that day I remembered, I could see the first star of the night. It was the same exact big bright star as the day I felt like I earned my place.

"I can't let myself die after making a promise like that, now, can I?"

I muttered this to myself, and Carbuncle let out a "*Squeak.*"

"You seem oddly happy."

"*Squeak?*"

"You little rascal."

I gently petted Carbuncle on his cute little head.

○

It was already nighttime by the time I made it back home.

As soon as my teacher saw my face, she said, "Oh? What's this?" with a somewhat happy tone to her voice. "I was expecting you to return with the countenance of a dead fish, but it seems the light has returned to your eyes."

"I'd like to imagine I never look like a fish."

I pouted as I said this and held out my no-longer-empty bottle. The tears of the doctor and his daughter had crystallized into two small shards that rattled at the bottom of the container. The two shards looked as if I had cut them from a diamond myself.

"Are these the tears of joy you were talking about?"

"Let's see here…," my teacher said, and held the bottle up to more closely examine its contents. "They are not, it seems," she said without hesitation. "These tears contain a mixture of joy and sadness. They are not tears of pure joy."

"So I can't use them to make a seed of life?"

"No. Not under normal conditions anyway."

She continued to closely examine the bottle after she said this. It was rare for my teacher, who could see through pretty much anything, to have this much interest in something.

"They are not tears of joy, but they are clear nonetheless. I sense incredible power beyond the norm."

"*Clear* as in see-through?"

"Yes. These tears are of pristine, good feelings. As clear as day."

"Is that why the bottle accidentally collected them, you think?"

"Perhaps."

My teacher looked happy when she said this.

"Um… You in a good mood?"

"You are a witch who can open the hearts of others."

"Opening people's hearts… Maybe that'd be useful if I was a surgeon."

"There is no need for sarcasm. I am trying to compliment you, my child."

"Why did you wait until I had a year left to tell me? You could've given me five or six years, or maybe…"

I couldn't find any more words to say after this escaped my mouth.

"Could you accomplish what you must if you had five or six years?"

"No…"

My teacher knew me well. She knew the more time I had, the more likely I was to spend it doing nothing. In fact, I wouldn't put it past myself to procrastinate until the very day I'd keel over as an old lady on that bench.

"Death's Decree doesn't show itself until a year before it is set to take effect. It isn't apparent that you are sick, nor that you will die when you turn eighteen, until then."

"Even for a powerful mage such as yourself?"

"Correct. There are no exceptions. It is a powerful curse that rewrites causality the moment it takes hold over its host. But even more importantly..."

My teacher smiled gently as she continued.

"I knew it was worth telling you, for the woman you've grown to be has the power to push back against your fate."

"Push back against fate..."

"So, Meg. What are you going to do?"

"What do you mean?"

"Will you curl up in a ball and let death's grip take hold over you, or will you pour what time you have left into the possibility of life? It's your decision to make."

I'd learned something that day: That I had aspirations I'd yet to fulfill and promises I needed to keep. That there were people who wanted me to live. That I needed to live for those important to me.

And that I was allowed to fight against my destiny.

"You know, this really is the worst birthday present ever." I raised my head. "I'll do it," I answered before I even knew it. "I'll accumulate the one thousand tears of joy you asked for."

When she heard me say this, my teacher gave me a big bold grin—even bolder than usual—as she looked at me. *That's the answer I was waiting for*, her eyes seemed to say.

"You should give it your all, Meg Raspberry. Your life depends on how you spend this next year."

* * *

I took a slow, deep breath.

"I know."

And that's all I said.

This is the story of a miracle performed by a young witch who was told she only had a year left to live.

Chapter 2:
A Day in the
Life of an
Apprentice
Witch

A witch in training had to wake up early. My eyes opened with the rise of the sun, not by habit but by instinct.

"I just wanna sleep..."

It was still a bit dark outside as I lugged my heavy limbs out of bed, and two little animals accompanied me: Carbuncle, the established familiar, and White-Owl.

Carbuncle was a familiar summoned by my teacher, but she passed him down to me after he appeared to take a liking to me.

White-Owl was a snowy owl I took in as a fledgling and turned into my familiar after finding the chick's mommy owl dead. According to my teacher, the color white was a symbol of the servants of God, but it meant little to me either way.

My teacher had tons of familiars, but these two were my own. They were both intelligent and capable of powerful magic—according to my teacher, at least.

"Both of your familiars are incredibly wise. They possess intellect far beyond your own."

"Hardy-har-har. You and your jokes."

My teacher didn't look like she was joking when she said this, but she couldn't possibly have been serious.

"Good morning, you two."

The two sat quietly while I petted them, each closing their eyes in bliss. Their fur and feathers were puffed up, almost like they were so comfortable that they could fall back asleep right there.

Waking them up again after their morning petting session was a part of my daily routine of witchery.

"Aaah-aaaaaah…"

Yawning loudly as I heated some water for the teakettle was also a part of the routine. With some tea on the stove, I headed for my teacher's study. Two firm knocks elicited the "Come in" I was used to hearing every morning.

"Excuse me."

Opening the door revealed my teacher, who was already nose-deep in a book with her reading glasses on. At what time she'd started reading was beyond me.

In fact, I wasn't even sure if I'd ever seen the Eternal Witch, Lady Faust, tired before. Perhaps being a first-class witch meant never sleeping. It was something I couldn't possibly fathom.

"Good morning, Meg."

"Good morning…"

"You need to speak more clearly in the—"

My teacher stopped speaking as soon as she turned to look at me.

"What happened? You're a mess."

"Heh, well, I was awakened by a vicious attack this morning…"

Saying this with the slightest bit of contempt in my voice had my two familiars hang their heads low in sorrow. My teacher shrugged in exasperation, suggesting she didn't approve of our morning antics.

"Here's your tea."

"Oh, thank you."

She took a sip, then let out a long exhale. Leaving her to her cup of tea, I fed all the small animals that were just waking up. They were my teacher's familiars, of which there were easily over a thousand. Though there was only about a third of them in the room that day, it was still an imposing number to behold.

The familiars always came to my feet when they were hungry. This part of my morning ritual never ceased to make me feel like a pet food dispenser. That's essentially all I was as I dropped seeds and corn kernels here and there for them to eat. They would eat up every last crumb, otherwise my teacher would get mad at them for leaving anything behind.

"Here's some food. Who's a good little woodland creature? You are! And you. And you, and you, and..."

Over the years of feeding and training the little tykes, I'd acquired all sorts of strange animal care techniques. Sometimes, I felt more like a zoo employee than I did an apprentice witch.

"Whew," I said after leaving the study and heading back to the kitchen. Animal-clad in White-Owl, who sat perched on my head, and Carbuncle, who sat in a similar position on my shoulders, I looked a bit odd as I prepared breakfast for us humans.

Bacon and eggs with a side of salad, a slice of bread, and some fruit for dessert. This was the same breakfast we'd had at the manor for as long as I could remember, and my teacher would always appear at the breakfast table right when I finished making it.

Mornings were always peaceful at the witch's manor.

"Meg."

"What's up?"

"I must focus on my work this morning, so I will leave the manor in your care."

"You got it. Did something happen?"

"Yes, in the United States. It has to do with a politician, and as the request for my help was made through the Council of Magic, I cannot ignore it."

"Wow, sounds complicated. I know zilch about politics."

"You really ought to make it a habit to watch the news. Magic is to know the flow of life, scoop up that flow, and mold it. That is part of our role as witches in this world."

"I think people like me are better suited to concerning themselves with what's for dinner than the world's politics."

"That I cannot disagree with."

"Just so you know, I'm inviting you to disagree with me when I self-deprecate."

We finished eating, and in line with her declaration, my teacher returned to her study, where she cooped herself up. She would only ever show herself at mealtimes when she was this busy. My teacher had the ability to hyperfocus beyond human comprehension to accomplish a difficult task at hand. I believe she told me at some point that *"Focus is the key to accomplishing any great task."*

Her words didn't strike a chord with me, though, given that I'd yet to accomplish anything great despite being the perfect example of focus.

"I guess we'd better get to cleaning."

"Hoot."

"Squeak."

White-Owl and Carbuncle were there to answer my words uttered to no one in particular.

○

"That's everyone."

I wore an apron and a bandanna wrapped around my head. I had a rag in one hand and a vacuum in the other. Geared head to toe and ready for battle, I stood before the entire manor's worth of familiars.

"Listen up, ladies and gents! My teacher put me in charge while she's not around, and we're gonna clean this place up until it's spotless! A filthy house sullies the soul! Do you hear me?!"

The little army of woodland creatures all squeaked, squawked, chirped, and yowled a *Ma'am, yes ma'am!*

We were ready.

"Begin!!"

I gave the orders, and the familiars all dispersed to clean at their posts. I fought with them on the front lines, vacuuming throughout the house with great vigor. I cleaned each room, which included mopping, organizing books, and then washing dishes and clothes. The manor was big, and I was going to need the familiars' help if I hoped to finish in any reasonable amount of time.

"I see you there! Put both of those front paws into your wiping! You need to use the loo? Hurry back to your nest, and make it quick! You two! Stop bickering! And you already had breakfast!"

It was an hour-long battle, but the tiny animals and I finally finished cleaning the entire manor.

"Whew, that was a workout."

I sprawled out on my desk, and Carbuncle wiped off my sweat while White-Owl massaged my shoulders by gently tapping on them with his talons.

These two really are the cutest.

I glanced over at the clock and saw that it was already eleven. I needed to give the familiars their lunch an hour before my teacher and I had ours, then I had to run to town for some errands. After that was magic practice and some studying before tending to the trees and plants in the Witch's Forest.

Maybe this is actually hell?

"Aaah… Nothing beats the smell of a fresh pot of tea," I said with a smile before taking a sip.

I breathed a long sigh of relief, satisfied with a job well done that morning. The familiars seemed satisfied as well. Teatime was always nice. I brought a table outside and had my tea in the garden. This was the only time I had for myself every day.

That's what it usually was for me anyway.

I calmly and quietly grabbed the table edge with both hands.

"The heck am I doing with my life?!"

Angrily flipping the table sent all my woodland familiar friends running and flying away. The table hit the ground a few feet away from me with a loud, satisfying *crash*, and the teapot that sat on top of it also cracked into several pieces. It didn't matter that I'd just finished cleaning.

"A week has passed already! I've spent this last week of my remaining one year of life cleaning this stupid manor!"

The fateful day I learned of my impending death was already a full week ago.

"Okay, riddle me this: How many tears am I gonna need a day if I want to live?! Answer!"

White-Owl hopped down to the ground, and with a "*Hoot*," scritched and scratched at the dirt with his talon, leaving some writing.

"Th-three tears a day...?"

Setting aside the fact that I'd gotten an actual answer from my owl, *I need to make three people so happy that they cried—every day...? All while taking care of my teacher's chores, which leave me with only a few hours each day...?*

"Waaait, wait, wait. It took me an entire day just to get my first two, and they weren't even *pure* tears of joy. So you're tellin' me I have to get one more on top of all that?"

White-Owl and Carbuncle both nodded.

"Argh!"

I ran my hands through my hair and fell to the ground, where I rolled around until I eventually banged my foot on the table I'd flipped over and screeched in pain.

This is bad. Veeery bad.

At this rate, I was as good as dead.

"Chores and errands eat up most of my day, so I have to do something about them... Which means I have to do something about that old hag—uh, ha...ppy teacher of mine."

I couldn't even picture it in my mind. Me, taking down one of the Seven Sages. A witch capable of wiping an entire country off the face of the planet, and I had to whack her before it was too late.

Heh, who am I kidding?

"Maybe I could poison her. Like with some wolfsbane, or a perfume that paralyzes her, or...a drug?"

I felt a jolt run through my body as this idea came to me.

Drugs! Medicine! That's it! I'll use medicine to make people cry! I can use it to control their hormones and up their adrenaline to kick their tear ducts into high gear. This just might solve all my problems in a single brew!

I needed to strike while the iron was hot. I ran and got my herbs, mixed them, and made a test potion. It didn't take long to come up with my first rendition.

"Now I just need someone to test this on..."

I glanced over at my familiars, and the two began to quiver. I tried to soothe them with a smile. It was a long, thin smile, like a crescent moon.

"There, there, babies. Everything'll be all right. You've got nothing to worry about. It's not like this will kill you or anything."

I said this to them while clutching Carbuncle by the scruff of his neck. My grip was gentle but firm enough for him to know I had no intention of letting him go, try as he may to escape. White-Owl pecked away at the back of my head as I did this.

"Well, what do ya want me to do?! I need a guinea pig for the sake of human advancement! C'mon, it's just one sip!"

I was wrestling around with my two familiars when I heard a voice call out, "What in the world are you doing?"

The three of us froze and turned our heads toward the source of the voice.

"Are you goofing off again today?"

It was my friend Fine standing in the doorway.

○

Fine Cavendish. She was a student who lived in Lapis and was a year younger than me. We'd known each other for more than ten years, and she was one of my best friends.

Fine had lovely facial features and lush blond hair, and she always dressed fashionably—although each article of clothing she wore was reasonably priced. It was easy to tell that she was raised well and had a good head on her shoulders. Especially compared to a witch in training who wore a floppy robe, tied her hair up in a bun to hide how disheveled it was, and never wore any makeup—not that such a character is a part of this story.

"What's all the hubbub about?"

"Oh, nothing. Just the teensy, *tiiiniest* little thing happened, but it doesn't matter anymore."

I needed Fine to let her guard down. I calmed my familiars and propped my table back up with the same crescent grin from earlier on my face.

"I was just about to make some delicious tea. Here, you can have some in my teacher's favorite cup."

"Wow, that's a really fancy cup."

I prepared the tea while Fine was distracted by the cup I'd set on the table. With elegant hands, I poured my friend the special brew I'd prepared earlier. My two familiars knew exactly what I was doing and watched with horror in their eyes.

"You didn't do something weird to this tea, did you?"

Fine took one look at the tea before shooting me a dubious

look. She sometimes made sharp, insightful realizations like this that showed how well she knew me.

"C-c'mon, who says no to free tea? You wanna fight?"

"You're acting strange..."

"It's really expensive tea, and I want you to try it. C'mon. C'mon, c'mon, c'moooooon."

"All right... If you insist..."

Though very suspicious of me and my cup of tea, she picked it up and lifted it to her lips. Slowly...the cup moved through the air, and just as it was about to hit her glossy lips—

"Hiyaaaaaah!!!" I stole the cup from her hands and threw it against the wall as hard as I could. The cup shattered into a thousand pieces, and tea splattered everywhere. "Bloody hell!! That really was Teacher's favorite cup!!!"

"Seriously? What are you doing?!"

I knew I'd never forget the face Fine made when I did that. I'd never seen someone so completely taken aback before.

"You were going to give me spiked tea?!"

"I'm really sorry. I hope you can forgive me. Pwetty pwease? Waaah."

I clung to her legs, begging for forgiveness, and Fine let out an exasperated sigh.

"Why in the world would you try to drug me?"

"Because I'm running out of options... I don't know what to do!"

I told Fine everything. That I only had a year left to live, and about the thousand tears of joy I needed to collect, and how despite all this, I'd spent the last week doing assistant work.

Fine thought I was joking at first, chuckling as she listened along, but the reality of my situation soon set in, and her expression became serious.

"Are you really going to die, Meg?"

"Yup, I guess I'm cursed."

"A curse… Can't Lady Faust just, I dunno, *uncurse* you?"

"Nope, she said she can't. She said this curse is like a chronic disease that I was born with."

"And that's why you need one thousand tears of joy. Making people cry tears of joy doesn't sound very easy."

"It really isn't. Look at this. It's the result of my first week. Two tears, and they aren't even of pure joy."

I passed my bottle of tears to Fine, and she looked at the two crystal shards with interest. At the bottom of the bottle were two of the tiniest shards imaginable. These were the clear crystal tears of two people.

"Wow, so these are the crystals. I don't know much about magic and all that stuff, but these sure are pretty. They seem clear, or pure, to me at least. It feels like there's nothing extra in them."

"I still don't really get it, either, what *pure* tears are."

I shook the bottle, and the tear shards rattled inside. I stared at my two shards, when I heard Fine say, "But…you're not the type to be satisfied with tears shed through medicine, I bet."

"You know me well."

"We've been friends for over ten years, after all."

"Yup. Maybe we should get married."

"I don't think we're *that* close."

"Awww…"

I was desperate, and Fine was both weirded out by me and sorry for me. She was right, though. I knew forcing the tears out of people with drugs wasn't going to work. My teacher said I needed to collect shards of *emotion*.

The tears shed by Dr. Hendy and Anna were extra special, and even if they weren't pure joy, they were shards of raw emotion. Tears earned from drugs and other underhanded methods certainly wouldn't be of emotion and likely wouldn't be suitable for a seed. And even if they did work, I wouldn't want that to be the foundation for my life.

"I'm at a loss here."

Fine chuckled at the sight of me in such deep thought.

"What's so funny?"

"Meg, you're so nice. You don't always have to make everything a joke. Maybe you should be a bit more honest with yourself."

"I don't wanna hear it. So when are we gonna have the wedding?"

"I'll pass."

A question popped into my mind while we shared in our fun banter.

"What brings you to the manor today anyway, Fine?"

Fine's expression became a bit awkward before she responded.

"What makes you think I came here for something?"

"Well, it's rare for you to come all the way here just to see me. So I'm sure there's something you want. You don't need to hold back with me; we're pals! Let's hear it. C'mon."

Hearing me say this, Fine showed some determination and continued.

"I'm actually here because I want to see Lady Faust about something."

○

My teacher had said she was busy that day, but I knew she would make time for Fine. The girl had been my best friend since we were little kids. There was no way my teacher would ever ignore her request.

I determined this a worthy cause before knocking on the door to her study, and I was beckoned with a "Come in." At first, I was expecting my teacher to be mad at the intrusion, but my anxiety turned out to be unwarranted.

"Thank you."

I let myself in and saw that my teacher was surrounded by a great wall of books and towering stacks of papers. In the middle of it all, she sat with a single sheet of paper before her. She may have been in the process of designing a spell circle.

"There's something I need to speak with you about…"

"It's about Fine, yes? Go ahead."

It wasn't clear when she'd realized Fine's presence, but she looked over at the door from where my friend peeked into the room. Fine felt my teacher's gaze and hurriedly entered the room with an "Ah yes!"

"L-Lady Faust. I-I'm sorry to bother you when you're so busy."

"It's all right, my dear. Tell me what it is you need."

"Th-thank you. So…"

"You want me to fix a clock?"

From her book fortress, my teacher looked at us with surprise, and Fine nodded yes with a bit of hesitation.

"I know it's an insignificant thing to ask someone of your stature, but my wristwatch broke, and the clockmaker said there's nothing he can do about it."

"Is that so? Well, let me see it."

"Here."

Fine took her wristwatch off and handed it to my teacher. I knew the watch well; she wore it all the time. There were nicks and scratches all over the watch, and it had spots here and there where the original color had faded. It didn't look like there was much that could be done to get it moving again, but although it no longer functioned as a watch, Fine still wore it.

My teacher examined the watch closely before sharing with us, "Your watch has lost all signs of Spirits."

"Spirits? Like from fairy tales?"

My teacher answered Fine. "Not quite like the ones you hear about in stories."

"Whether the item in question is organic or inorganic, so long as it serves a purpose, it harbors Spirits. In the East, they view such artifacts as being inhabited by the Spirits, whether it be the souls of the deceased or their many gods or goddesses. These Spirits move the things they inhabit—think of them as a power source."

"And you're saying that my watch has lost its power source?"

My teacher nodded in response to Fine's question and then turned her look to me.

"You should know better than most, Meg."

"Huh? Well, yeah..."

Spirits weren't something you could normally see. This went for witches and wizards as well, but for a mage as powerful as my teacher, she could determine whether they were present. The reason a mage of my teacher's caliber would turn to me at a moment like this was because, well, I was born with the ability to instinctively know whether there were Spirits in any given place. The magic in my eyes was powerful, a rare trait to be born with; or so I'd been told.

I looked at Fine's watch, and it was as my teacher said. It was void of all Spirits. The better description was that there *were* Spirits there, but they showed no sign of activity. It was as if they'd lost their life and were in the middle of a long, long slumber.

Their slumber told the story of a watch that had fulfilled its role and lived out the extent of its life.

"So I suppose that means my watch is—"

Fine spoke with a sad expression, but my teacher cut her off. "Now, let's not jump to conclusions."

"Meg, take Fine to Geppetto's shop."

"Geppetto?"

Fine repeated the name with a bit of confusion, and I nodded.

"He's a clockmaker in town. His shop is all run-down and dilapidated. It makes you wonder how he's still in business."

"Geppetto's shop is in business because he does good work. Artisans skilled at their craft can at times breathe life into things. Geppetto may be able to fix your watch, even though the other clockmakers have deemed it irreparable."

"Really…?"

"We'll see. You may as well give it a shot, even if the chances are slim. If that is all you need, then please take your leave. I'm very busy."

Fine and I hurried out of the study, and she breathed a sigh of relief.

"No matter how many times I see Lady Faust in person, I'll always be nervous when I meet her. She seemed really busy, and I half expected her to get mad at us for interrupting her about a watch."

"My teacher doesn't get upset at townspeople. She's been livid with me before, though, like when I tried to cook one of her familiars."

"Well, in that case, you definitely deserved it."

My teacher was one of the Seven Sages. Even though she was always busy with something, I'd never seen her refuse to listen to a request from one of the townsfolk before. Witches were meant to help people. This was the ancient way, and my teacher observed those teachings, which meant helping people when they needed help, even when she was busy.

Whether it be a child or elder, male or female, a politician or a housewife, my teacher treated everyone the same.

Whether the request be to fix something or for the sake of world peace, my teacher treated each request with the same importance.

This may have been the reason she was so popular and a great witch.

"Let's go. If there's one thing Mr. Geppetto's great at, it's fixing watches. I bet he won't throw in the towel like the rest of the town's clockmakers."

"Really? I hope he can fix it..."

"But why not just buy a new one? You can get a really nice watch for cheap nowadays. You don't have to worry about a digital watch stopping on you like that, or maybe you could get one by a famous designer."

"Yeah, I know. But how should I put this...? I still want to use this watch a bit more. I'm really attached to it."

"Oh? You're attached to it, eh...?"

"You were never one to get attached to things like this, Meg."

I didn't really understand the idea of being attached to something like a mug, cup, or watch. Either way, I concluded that the watch was special to Fine.

I hadn't recognized exactly what this watch meant for Fine yet.

○

The clockmaker we went to had a small shop at the far end of the town market. It had a retro feel...which was putting it nicely; the place was a dump. Most people probably didn't even know it was a clockmaker's shop.

But I knew it was. The old man running it loved clocks more than anyone ever had.

We opened the door, and a gentleman with a white beard and round glasses greeted us.

"Hey, Mister. You've got a customer."

"Well, well. If it isn't the disciple. Welcome. It's rare for you to bring a friend with you."

"Oh, this isn't just any friend. She's my *best friend for life*, or BFFL, if you will."

"Biffle, eh? That's an interesting name. Judging by her looks, I would've guessed she's English, but I'm guessing she must be from the south?"

"...Does *biffle* sound like a Spanish name to you?"

While I gave old Geppetto a stare-down, Fine looked around his shop.

"I apologize for the sudden intrusion. I am Meg's friend, Fine. But wow. Just look at all these clocks... I didn't know there was a clock shop here."

I nodded along with Fine's words of awe.

"This shop is still in business despite looking like one big dustbin."

"Ha-ha-ha, you were never one to leave anything unsaid. Ha-ha-ha."

His eyes aren't laughing.

Whether it be wristwatches, alarm clocks, or cuckoo clocks, the shop's walls were covered in every clock and watch imaginable. It was easy to tell they were all thoroughly cared for, with each clock being exactly on time. Each clock also had a healthy number of Spirits inhabiting it. This wasn't the case for a more amateur clockmaker. This man was a true artisan.

"So what brings you to my shop today?"

"My friend here wants you to take a look at her watch."

Fine handed the older gentleman her watch, and he adjusted his spectacles accordingly with a "Let's take a look-see.

"Well this is quite the specimen you have here. It's a very old-fashioned military watch from Germany."

"You can tell?"

"Well, I *am* a clockmaker. Whoever made this watch did a good job. You can tell by the handiwork with its finer parts. Germany has a lot of skilled clockmakers, and the craftsmanship that went into this fine watch is very evident."

"So...do you think you can fix it?"

"We'll have to see about that. I can't tell without taking a closer look. But I'll need more time before I can get to it. As you can see, I am my shop, so I need to be ready for other customers when they come. Let me put this away for later."

"Oh yeah? Well, how about this…?"

A few minutes later.

"How did I end up doing this?"

With an exhausted expression, Fine let out a big sigh. She and I were sitting at the shop's front desk, waiting for customers, while Mr. Geppetto worked on her watch.

From the shop's storefront window, I could see the peaceful town. The shop was at the far end of the shopping district, so there weren't many people who walked by, especially compared to the town center. Fine seemed dissatisfied with the turn of events, with her elbow on the table propping up her head on her fist.

"Meg."

I was staring off into space outside a window when Fine said my name.

"Are you really going to die?"

"That's what I've been told."

"How are you okay with this?"

"I'm not *okay* with it. It just doesn't feel real yet. You know I'm bad at worrying about things."

"You always were a big ball of positivity."

"I'd go as far as to say that it may be my very best trait—"

I said this with a bit of a grin but was shocked by the expression on Fine's face when I turned toward her. She was biting her lip and appeared as if she was about to burst into tears. Her eyes were like a dam that was ready to burst.

I panicked and looked for something to change the

conversation, but the only things on the walls were a whole bunch of apathetic clocks.

"Uh, Fine? I-is something the matter?"

"Of course there is! I'm sad about your death. Why did you have to die, Meg…?"

"I'm not dead *yet*!"

Fine was about to cry just at the thought of my passing. I wished she wouldn't off me in her mind, though. Thinking back on it, this was how she'd always been. She had a good head on her shoulders, but she was very compassionate, empathetic, and nice.

This is just like her facial expression when we first met, I fondly recalled.

Fine and I first met when we were small children. I'd gotten into a fight with some kids back in town and was beaten and bruised.

"Are you okay?"

I was watching the sun set in the park, biting my lip in frustration after the fight, when Fine approached me. She wiped my bleeding nose and put a bandage on one of my scrapes.

"You're bleeding… Those meanies…"

As she patched me up, she was crying as though it were her with the scrapes and bruises.

"Why are you crying?"

"'Cause it looks like it hurts…"

There I was, holding back my tears, but Fine cried for me instead, and I remember liking her almost immediately for it.

"Hey, what's your name?"

"Fine…"

"You don't have to cry, Fine… I want you to smile."

I wiped her tears away, which surprised her at first, but she then exclaimed, "Okay!"

With tears still welling in her eyes, she'd given me a big smile.

I'd gone home to tell my teacher about what happened, and she'd softened her usual stern expression and spoke in a gentler tone.

"Meg, you need to remember this day. People always forget the good things and instead let the bad things scar them. You're the opposite, though. You always forget the bad things and hold on to what brought you happiness. Never let yourself forget about the child who helped you today."

"I won't, Teacher."

I think Fine stopping and using her new handkerchief to help me with my wounds kept me from hating humanity. Incidentally, I got back at the kids who bullied me by turning their bathwater into poo while they were still in it. I know it was a bit much, so we'll save that story for another day.

Fine was still nice, just like she'd been when we were children. I was sure the only reason she made an effort to hold her tears back like this was because she hadn't forgotten what I told her on the day we met.

"Don't look so sad, Fine. You're cutest when you're smiling. And it's not like I'm dead yet, nor do I even plan on dying."

"Meg…"

While tears weren't running down her cheeks, she was sniffling audibly. It was a shame to see such a beautiful girl a crying mess. I found a cloth and used it to gently wipe Fine's nose.

"I want to be there when you get into and graduate from college. And for your wedding, and to see your grandchildren. I'm gonna punch your fiancé at least once when I meet him, though."

"What are you, my mum?"

The two of us shared a chuckle.

"Was that a handkerchief you wiped my tears with, by the way?"

"No, it was an old rag."

"..."

○

Within less than thirty minutes, old man Geppetto reappeared from the back of the shop.

"Sorry to keep you waiting, ladies."

"How's it look?"

"I'm sorry, but it's simply this watch's time."

The old man shook his head.

"I thought maybe I could switch some parts out, but the hands and glass are in very bad shape and too old to find replacements. Seeing how long this watch has been used for, I doubt it's possible to repair it."

"Whoa, slow down, Doc. You're making the watch sound like a piece of junk here. You wouldn't want to hurt its feelings, wouldja?"

"I'm just telling it like it is..."

"You gotta be careful about the words you use. Girls are delicate creatures. Especially the pretty ones. Like me."

"Heh, is that right?"

"What're ya laughin' for?"

The clockmaker and I were enjoying our banter, when we both heard Fine say, "I thought that would be the case..."

She was looking down at the ground like a puppy that had just gotten in trouble, and we both fell silent.

"This watch belonged to my grandfather. It's a shame I won't be able to use it anymore."

Hearing Fine say this reminded me that the watch had been given to her by her beloved grandfather before he passed away.

He was a warm and gentle man, but he passed away when we were still children. My teacher and I went to his funeral. I could still remember watching Fine cling to his body in the coffin, wailing at the top of her lungs. It wasn't often you saw someone crying so hard for someone else like that.

"I can tell this watch is very important to you."

Geppetto said this quietly as he looked at the watch in his hand.

"There are lots of spots that have been repaired, and the wristband has been replaced. This watch should've stopped a long time ago, but it was still ticking until now. I'm sure your watch had an incredible life and that it was glad it ended up with you."

"Thank you..."

"It's strange, but after so many years of handling clocks, I've come across a handful of watches that kept on ticking far longer than they probably should have. I've always felt this was the watch's way of answering the people who care so much for it. I'm sure your watch felt the same about you."

"The watches respond to people's kindness..."

I'd never grasped the idea of getting attached to an object. This was because I didn't have anything that had memories attached to it. Watching Fine, though, I felt like I understood what it meant to have an item or trinket that was important to a person. I'm sure her watch was like a good luck charm for her. It was what remained of her dear late grandfather. I was sure she remembered him when she had it on her, whenever she felt happy or sad. It must've been like he was there with her.

"I might not be able to use it as a watch anymore, but I guess I can still keep it to remember him by..."

Fine said this with a smile, but there was something hidden behind her expression. I'm sure she was saying this more to herself than to us, as her way of telling herself it was time to give up.

Is there anything I can do for my friend? I thought for a few moments before eventually tapping Fine on the shoulder.

"Hey, Fine."
"Yeah?"
"I have an idea."

"A mourning *what*?"

Orange leaves fell from the trees around us in the town square where Fine watched with wide eyes as I drew a spell circle on the ground with a branch.

"A mourning ritual. It's something witches used to do to thank certain items that they'd used for a long time. Think of it as a way to say good night. You know how the Spirits inside your watch have used up all their energy and are now in an eternal rest? We're gonna do a ritual to tuck them in tight for eternity."

"Wow, I've never heard of that before."

"The idea that all things harbor Spirits is a very witch-and-wizard sort of concept. Sometimes, we borrow their power to perform magic. Think of this as our way of thanking spirits who've fulfilled their duties."

"Sounds kind of religious."

"Well, magic is chock-full of religious ideology."

I etched out a small circle on the ground, then a larger one around that. This made a donut shape where I would formulate my spell. I had to pick and choose where I would cut off each verse to fill them with meaning, verses that I would later chant.

An intrigued Fine watched from over my shoulder as I scratched out my magic circle on the ground.

"I love the little shapes you use in your spells. They're so pretty."

"Are you talking about runes?"

"They're called runes?"

Runes were a special alphabet that used different combinations of lines to formulate its characters. Each individual character had its own meaning and could also be used for things like fortune telling. Runes had been created long ago when, unlike now, civilization was more in tune with nature. Thus, runes bore the power to activate the laws of nature.

"Do you know them all by heart?"

"I know a few alphabets, like runes and the signs for the twelve zodiac signs. I have the characters of the Theban alphabet that are used for spells memorized. I don't know what they actually mean, though."

"Wow..."

Fine was clearly impressed, though something about the way she was staring at me felt a bit off.

"What?"

"It's just, uh...I didn't know you were so smart."

"You're acting like that's not a given? You want me to smack you?"

In this way, she kept me entertained while I finished my circle. Once it was complete, I placed a handkerchief in the middle, then set Fine's watch on it.

"What happens next? It's not gonna burst into flames or something, is it?"

"Relax. You don't think I'd do something like that to my best friend's precious watch, do you?"

"That's why I'm asking... I mean, you did try to drug your best friend earlier..."

"Cut the chitchat! I've got a spell to chant!"

I snapped my fingers, and Carbuncle dismounted my shoulder while White-Owl, who'd been flying above, joined him on the ground. My two familiars and I formed a triangle around the magic circle. The three of us were going to be a catalyst for the magic, which would travel through us evenly.

As I held my hand over the magic circle, the immediate vicinity surrounding us grew dark, and the runes began to faintly glow—a magic reaction. It was time for me to begin the twelve-verse chant I'd written into the circle.

"Worker Spirits both kind and true—come to me in your eternal rest—so that you may begin anew."

A swirl of wind lifted up the fallen leaves around the magic circle as I chanted, like they were dancing along with the ritual.

"For two lifetimes of work so resolute—I pay respect so absolute."

The watch was then enveloped in a faint glow, and from its center emerged a small orb of beautiful, clear light. It looked like a tiny sun. This was the group of Spirits that had fulfilled their duty to the item they inhabited.

"With gratitude deep and sincere—into life's cycle I return you here."

The orb of light shot high up into the sky, bringing the dancing leaves up with it. The leaves flittered and fluttered around the orb, only to then be blown around the park by a gentle breeze that also seemed to center around the orb. Fine let out a "Whoa..." in awe at the spectacular light show.

"I have but one wish—for when you finish your quest—I pray you return—to the place you knew best."

The light then began to grow larger. It was time for the finale.

"Now return to the cycle."

* * *

With my final verse, the light exploded, spreading out in every direction without making a sound. It expanded out toward the ground, the trees, and to the heavens before eventually dissipating. Ambient light then returned to the surrounding area, and the hustle and bustle of the town square could once more be heard.

"I-is it over?"

"Yup."

"What happened?"

"I returned the dormant Spirits in your watch to nature. These Spirits can then be reborn and then come back to you in the form of a new item."

I smiled as I said this.

"That new item will find its way to you, and you'll have something new to remember your favorite grandfather by."

"Meg…"

Though it wasn't possible to bring someone back from the dead, nor could items used to the extent of their life spans be fixed, in this way, it was possible for two souls to meet again. This was what my teacher called the flow of life.

"Hey, Fine. Your watch may be broken, but the memories it has of your grandpa will never disappear."

I looked at Fine.

"The Spirits we just sent off were full of memories of both you and your grandpa. So I'm sure you'll meet them again sometime. The Spirits cherish you two just as much as you cherished each other."

Fine's lips quivered.

"Thanks…!"

A tear ran down her cheek, and I felt the light jingle of a single shard within the bottle at my waist.

"I didn't think I would cry like that."

Fine said this as we walked back to town. I was petting Carbuncle, who sat on my shoulder.

"Something about that light made me remember so many things at once."

"About your grandpa?"

"Yeah, about how we used to play and what we used to eat together. Or how he used to pat me on the head to make me feel better when I got hurt. All these memories came surging up at once."

"You were always a grandpa's girl."

"The light that came out of his old watch... It sure was a gentle light, wasn't it?"

"I think so, too."

It was more than likely that the Spirits harbored by the watch carried the memories of two lifetimes.

"I think I'm gonna go get a new watch."

On our way back, we passed old man Geppetto's watch shop, where Fine stopped in her tracks and stared through the window.

"Oh? Something catch your eye already? I say go for it."

"Yeah. Tell me which Spirits match best with me."

"You got it! I'll choose some that'll bring you happiness."

I knew Fine would be okay. She had me as her friend, after all.

○

"I'm baaack!"

I'd helped Fine pick out a new watch before heading home, and I was greeted with a "Welcome home" by my teacher.

"Did everything go well with Fine's watch?"

"I think we figured it out. So, uh, what are you doing?"

"Oh, I'm just looking for something."

"Really? Why not rev up the ole *All-Seeing Eye*?"

"You mustn't rely on magic to overcome all of life's trifles, Meg. It is important to solve some problems using your own hands."

"You're so stubborn."

As I said this, a question popped into my mind.

"Hey, Teacher. Why did you send me and Fine to the clockmaker's?"

"Why, you ask?"

"Well, I'm sure you knew old man Geppetto couldn't fix the watch, so I thought it was strange that you sent us there in the first place."

A kind smile appeared on my teacher's face.

"As I just said, you mustn't always rely on magic. I hadn't looked into yours or Fine's future at that moment. I knew Fine still had hope for her watch, and I simply thought Geppetto perhaps could discern the watch's true value and provide the desired conclusion. I also—"

"Also what…?"

"Thought it may be a good opportunity to teach a foolish witch the true value of material things."

"A foolish witch? You shouldn't be so harsh on yourself…"

"I'm talking about you, you dolt!!"

The true value of material things. It wasn't the price something could be bought or sold for but the memories and affection a person had for that item.

I heard a *rattle* as I pondered over this. It was the shards of tears jingling around in the bottle I had fastened to my belt. I took it off my belt and waved it in front of my eyes.

There was a new tear, bringing my collection to a grand total of three.

"The true value of things…"

The light of the setting sun shone down on the bottle as I held it, causing the three tear shards to glimmer brilliantly. All three tears belonged to people who were important to me. This wasn't something that could be bought with money; it was something that was precious to me and me only.

"I bet this will become my most treasured possession."

I murmured this to myself, and Carbuncle looked up at me with a "*Squeak*" and White-Owl, a "*Hoot*." They both looked happy, and something about the woodland pair felt extra precious to me that day.

"I must ask, Meg. Have you seen my cup? You know the one; I always use it."

"Uh, that's what I'm saying… You should whip out the ole All-Seeing Eye and…"

I began to trail off mid-sentence. Should she use her Eye, she would find out in an instant her cup's unfortunate fate, and that it was my fault.

The cup had smashed into a million pieces when I threw it on the ground to prevent Fine from drinking the tea laced with tear-inducing magical herbs I almost tested on her.

"It's quite strange, really. I could've sworn I left it here. You didn't place it anywhere, did you?"

"Welp, look at the time! I'd better feed the familiars!"

As soon as I changed the subject, a hungry horde of tiny woodland creatures came out from the nooks and crannies of the manor and gathered at my feet as I left the room, with White-Owl closing the door behind me.

Ever since I learned I was destined to die, little by little, every day was starting to feel different. Though I didn't spend my days any differently than I usually did, the tears I gathered gave my life a new meaning, taught me new values, and earned me the tears of my dear friends.

A day like this was just a regular day for me now that I knew I was going to die.

And it was an important day I knew I could never forget.

Chapter 3:
Wisdom
Visits from
the East

It was early morning, and things were quiet as I munched on some salad and bread.

"It's a misuse of government funds, I say. Our taxes would be much better used rebuilding this here manor."

"Squeak."

"Hoot."

This was usually where the eldest member of the manor would reprimand me from the side for my dillydallying at breakfast, but I didn't have to worry about that today.

Instead, I had the luxury of sipping on some tea next to my two favorite familiars as I watched some television. The news was full of frightening stories lately. Entirely unknown to those who lived in this peaceful town of ours, there was a world of despair out there—or at least that's the picture the news painted.

I'd recently made it a point to watch the news more. It wasn't something I usually paid attention to, but with a certain old hag breathing down my neck about keeping up with current events... My teacher wanted me to do it, so I did. Seeing as she was one of the, you know, Seven Sages and all, I guess she didn't want her apprentice to be some country bumpkin.

"What use is any of this anyway? I wanna watch my shows."

Staring uninterestedly at the screen, I continued to chow down on snacks, when something interesting happened to come on.

"In recent news, the International Magic Conference, overseen by the esteemed Seven Sages, concluded just forty-eight hours ago.

Among the pressing topics addressed was the growing concern over the ecological impact of magical activities. As a proactive measure, two representatives from the Seven Sages are now on their way to a location in Central America believed to be bearing the brunt of such magical disturbances—"

"Huh? The conference is already over?"

I glanced at my smartphone. Most people thought witches lived a more traditional lifestyle, so it usually caught them off guard when I'd whip out my phone. I bet they thought we used magic to contact each other. Could you imagine, though? It could take a few minutes to chant a spell that would even come close to doing what a smartphone did in mere seconds. The public didn't realize that their modern culture had already surpassed the magic arts.

I unlocked my phone and checked if there were any messages from my teacher but found nothing. She had attended the International Magic Conference that was held in North America.

"Meg, I shall be leaving the manor for a while."

A week prior, my teacher approached me about her trip. I was in the living room reading up on a magic formula at the time. It wasn't rare for my teacher to leave the manor for work. On the occasions when she would be gone for a few days or more, she would let me know beforehand.

"Where to this time?"

"North America. The Seven Sages will be assembling. There is a lot of work to be done, so I believe this conference may drag on for quite some time."

"Do you reckon it'll be on the telly?"

"I'm sure the news will pick it up. It isn't uncommon for our conferences to deal with international issues. There may also be changes to the rules regarding magic. The world is watching us mages, after all."

"Wow, must be nice."

Save for one member in particular, it was rare for any of the Seven Sages to appear on television. This was why such an event always drew so much attention.

"I wanna be on television someday. I think my beauty would captivate all the boys around the world."

"I believe your beauty would be better kept to yourself."

"What do you mean by that?"

"Understand that this will not be a vacation for me. I will be locked up in a conference hall for several sleepless days. You're welcome to go in my stead if you so wish."

"Ha-ha, methinks 'tis a most excellent notion!"

"Speak in a way that makes sense."

"Sorry. You don't need to worry about me, though. What's five, six days? I could last two months, even a year and be just peachy!"

"Perhaps, though I doubt the manor would last in that situation."

"What do you mean by that?"

It had been a week since my teacher left me with those words. I thought she'd be back around today, ready to talk my ear off with complaints about the conference, but evidently, the conference was already long over.

"Welp, I guess my short break is just gonna be that much longer."

As I mumbled this to myself, my eyes shifted to the second place setting of fresh bread and eggs I'd prepared for her return.

"I wonder if it would be wrong to eat two breakfasts..."

My idle musing echoed throughout the empty manor.

* * *

Much like the proverbial bolt out of the blue, however, it was always the most peaceful of times when happenings reared their ugly heads. In this case, it was early in the morning of the next day when the bolt struck.

The sun wasn't even up yet. I was still asleep, snug in my bed, when there was a commotion in the front hall. At first, I assumed it was two of the many woodland familiars getting into a spat, but the creaking of the front door opening quickly dispelled this guess. I squinted as I looked at the door, where light from outside crept in.

"Hmm? *Yaaawn.* Lemme sleep just a bit more..."

"Wake up. That's an order."

Drool was making its way from my open mouth onto my pillow when I felt something on my face.

"Huh? What's that?"

It was the bottom of a foot, and the second my mind processed it, my nose registered the incredible stench coming from it.

"That smells awful! What are you—? *Eugh! Oeugh!!*"

I fled to the corner of my room and started gagging. Then someone called out, "Well, excuse me! They don't smell that bad!"

Slowly, I looked up to see the owner of the smelly feet, and...

"You have some nerve."

...a woman stood there, wearing a pointed witch's hat and a black robe.

○

"I am Inori. Would you know me as the Wise Witch of the East?"

"Wise Witch...?"

I racked my brain, the Wise Witch, just like the Eternal Witch, was the title of one of the Council of Magic's Seven Sages.

"That's right, I'm the Wise Witch, Inori. One of the Seven Sages, at your service."

"Huh, you don't say."

My doubts weren't unwarranted, seeing as I'd heard the Wise Witch was over one hundred years old. The woman before me had wavy black hair and a perfect nose. She wore an open-shouldered, tightly fitted dress with slits here and there exposing her bare skin. She looked, at best, twenty-four or -five—far too young to be a Sage. I'd heard of witches with enough power to extend their life and alter their appearance, and in terms of power, I could tell just by looking at her that Inori had unimaginable power at her disposal.

"So what brings the Wise Witch to our humble abode?"

"Haven't you been watching the news? About the Seven Sages' inspection? There is an inspection being conducted on the impact of magical energy on the environment, and your teacher is the one overseeing it."

"Yeah…"

According to Inori, my teacher went to a part of the world that had a high concentration of magic. It wasn't uncommon for places like this to have poor cell phone reception due to the high magic density, which explained why I hadn't heard from her.

"Since it will take her a while to complete the inspection, your teacher wanted me to come check on the house."

"What?! I'm seventeen! I can take care of myself! She shouldn't treat me like a child!"

"It sounded like she was more worried about the house than you, per se."

"Oh… Right…"

Inori continued, "So I'll be spending the next few days with you," before patting the copious luggage behind her with her hand. There were three full-size trunk suitcases. She must've been an inexperienced traveler, because the businessmen and women seen running to and from the airports had at most a small roller on them.

"That's fine, Inori. I'd just like to ask one thing first."

"What's that?"

"Could you please wash your feet? They smell atrocious."

"I could end you right now if I wanted to."

Getting back to the subject at hand…

While Inori was busy wiping her feet with a towel, I sighed.

"Can you believe my teacher, though? She could've sent me a message before she went into the reception dead zone."

"She was afraid of what you'd do if you knew she wasn't coming back anytime soon."

"Ha-ha-ha. What could I do? Ha-ha-ha-ha."

What am I going to do? There's nothing to do! Except maybe test a few new spells on some of her defenseless familiars.

"Were you the one who brewed these herbs?"

As I schemed to myself, Inori was looking through my medicine cabinet with curiosity.

"Oh, yeah. How did you know?"

"Because Grandma Faust doesn't study medicine anymore."

"That's true."

My teacher was well-versed in many schools of magic, and this made her busy. This was especially true as of late due to her intense focus on time magic research. The research I was doing on medicine and plants was something I'd taken over for her.

"This smells nice."

"Right? That's a new recipe. It's filled with nourishment for your body, too. I bet you're tired from the council meeting. Would you like some tea?"

"That would be wonderful."

Herbal teas were my specialty. My teacher liked the tea I made as well and asked for some every morning. The color of this brew was close to black tea, but I could change it depending on which herbs I used.

"It tastes as good as it smells."

"I've added some black tea to enhance the flavor. That herb can be mixed with this one to make it more fragrant, and through the power of magic, I can make a good cup of tea."

Inori happily drank my tea as I gave her my little spiel about it.

"Oh? You seem quite capable. Do you have a witch name yet? Seeing as you're the Eternal Witch's apprentice, I wouldn't be surprised if you had one already."

Powerful mages earned witch and wizard names, and for those who practiced magic, these names were common sense. Just like the Eternal Witch for my teacher and the Wise Witch for Inori, it was a symbol of recognition passed on by the Council of Magic. Having a witch name meant you were both a powerful and competent witch.

"No way. I'm as *in-training* as they come."

"Is that something to be proud of?" Inori was a bit taken aback by the confidence with which I spoke, and with a wry grin, repeated, "A witch in training…" For whatever reason, it felt like there was a deeper meaning behind her saying this.

"Hey, I'd like to see more. You cultivate your own herbs here, right? Do you have your own plot?"

"We do. I'm tending a garden in the Witch's Forest just outside of here. It's closer to a hobby than an actual garden, though."

"Show it to me. Your garden."

"You got it. I actually wanted to go there today anyway."

"Are you going to pick something?"

"Yes, something for your feet. I think mint would do you wonders."

"Do they still smell...?"

○

The manor my teacher and I lived in was tucked into the Witch's Forest. These woods were a special place where I managed the magical energy and took care of the animals and plants. The soil was kept healthy through balanced magical energy levels, allowing for springlike temperatures throughout the year, and with plenty of healthy soil available, it was possible to harvest certain plants that wouldn't normally grow around these parts. There was also a large population of animals coexisting with the plants. I had to be sure none of the animals were dangerous, though, as the townsfolk of Lapis liked to stroll through these woods.

Inori walked alongside me, happily humming a tune as we meandered through the forest.

"You sure seem happy."

"I'm elated that boring conference is over. The air here is pristine; it feels great."

"Those conferences must be pretty difficult, I imagine?"

"They sure are. They last for days and run late into the night, with a plethora of topics to handle—most of which are either irregular in nature or without definitive conclusions. You should know all about this, though, seeing as you're an apprentice to one of the Seven Sages?"

"My teacher doesn't like to talk too much about work..."

"I see..."

Inori scratched her cheek, seemingly unsure of how to continue.

"She probably just doesn't want you to worry about her. It's nothing to fret over."

"When's she gonna come home?"

"Who knows? She's handling a real emergency. But since it's Grandma Faust we're talking about, I'm sure she'll figure it out and be home before you know it."

"You think so…?"

"You're worried about your teacher, aren't you?"

"Who, me? No way."

"What do you mean 'no way'? You should've seen the sad look you just had on!"

"It's just a shame to think that my break will come to an end…"

"Then why did you look upset when you mentioned her not telling you about her work?!"

"That was me trying not to yawn. Did I look sad?"

"It's not something to yawn about!"

With an astounded look in her eyes, Inori shook her head at me in disbelief and said, "You're quite difficult to read."

"I'm sure you're tired from the conference."

"I'm more tired from talking to you about it!"

There were many medicinal herbs from the East and West, as well as herbs used for fragrance, being grown in the Witch's Forest—each growing at an accelerated rate with incredible vibrancy. My main job was to manage the soil and magical energy levels in the forest. It wasn't to say that I left the herbs to their own devices, but there wasn't much work that needed to be done in terms of taking care of them. Healthy, bountiful soil was all they needed to grow well. All I had to do was thin the forest out here and there.

Inori squatted down and felt the soil at the plants' roots to check their condition for herself.

"These are thoroughly managed."

"I have to maintain the magic levels every day. It's quite the workload."

"Your teacher leaves it all to you?"

"Yes. You know how packed her schedule is, after all."

"Let's see here. The mulch quality and the amount of magic in the soil are both up to speed. You could probably grow anything here with how well it's being maintained. You have quite the green thumb on you."

"Darn tootin'! This here's my farm, ma'am."

My best farmer impression was lost on Inori, who just seemed confused. This was something of a letdown for me—I had confidence in that impression, too.

"Having an eye for soil is a powerful asset. Even more so now, seeing as how things have gotten strange lately, with the climate and environment changing so much. You'll be able to find a good job with a talent like that."

"That's nice to hear, but what do you mean?"

"People have had too much of an impact on the environment. They've polluted the air and cut down the forests, altering how the land was supposed to look. Despite this, the leaders of the world think they can use magic to fix what they've broken."

Lots of work the Seven Sages dealt with was environmental issues and research they were tasked with by the many governments of the world. One of the main issues being researched was the impact of magic on living beings and the consequences of that impact. It was thought that magic caused rare species to go extinct, drove animals mad, and warped the environment. They often talked on the news about how the world's deserts were expanding due to this.

"When deforestation removes plants from a given habitat, magic loses the channel through which it takes root into the ground. This results in that area's magic needing to find a new host, usually in the largest nearby life-form. The influx of magic focused on one individual often brings about changes. For example, the individual may consume weaker life-forms it previously didn't and change the balance of nature in the area."

Inori explained everything there was to the abnormal phenomenon without skipping a beat.

"The collection of magic gives a being power, but power isn't simply something that can be gained. Power that is too great for its vessel can cause imbalance within it, resulting in a rampage. It's a mage's job to maintain the balance of nature. If you gained power, what would you do with it?"

"I would use it to acquire wealth and fame, then create a harem of beautiful men to heed my every whim."

"You're not a great vessel, then."

Inori sighed in disbelief.

"Listen, if an animal eats a plant or fruit that has amassed large quantities of magic, it will absorb that magic into its body. This will make it attack people. In the East, we've experienced a gruesome bear attack that resulted in the death of several women who lived in the nearby village. There will be more attacks like this as the problem worsens. The animals will go in and out of villages, turning into monsters."

"Wow…"

By changing an ecosystem too much, or using spells that were too powerful, the balance of magic in a given area was disturbed. The Wise Witch of the East shared with me that this was slowly beginning to alter the life in those areas.

Needless to say, it was a very serious conversation.

"I'm not good at thinking about difficult things. You never know when you're gonna die. Life is short, and I think it should be lived to its fullest."

"What would *living life to its fullest* mean for you, Meg?"

"A couple of beers, a nice cigar, a delicious spread, and a beautiful woman."

"Oh, so you're a middle-aged man."

○

We eventually made it to the part of the forest I used for growing medicinal herbs. I'd enchanted the area with a spell that amplified the component of fresh lemongrass that kept bugs and other pests away.

The area had lavender, bay leaf, and arugula among many other herbs growing throughout it. That wasn't all; deeper in the garden, there were Eastern medicinal plants as well.

Seeing this spot, Inori let a "Wow" escape her lips. "You've done well for yourself. These are some sizable herbs, and you can smell how potent they all are. Not to mention the variety."

"I add more and more every year. This includes plants my teacher asks for, some I want to use for my own experiments, and herbs needed by the townspeople. They grow fast thanks to the quality of soil here."

I shared this as I plucked the mint we'd come here for. Mint was a virile herb that could be left alone and still thrive. In fact, planting mint in someone's garden was considered vandalism by plant enthusiasts because of its ability to take over a plot.

This was why I needed to be careful where I planted it when adding it to my forest garden. If it made its way to any of the other plants, it would quickly take over their seedbeds. I used magic to dampen its breeding power, but all it took was one seed to get loose for it to wreak havoc on another plant.

As I carefully collected the mint I needed, I found myself recalling the past. My mint held some memories.

Maintaining the magic levels of the Witch's Forest was one of the first tasks my teacher entrusted me with when I was very young.

"Here we are, Meg Raspberry. You'll be in charge of taking care of the forest from now on."

"I don't wanna."

I said no to the job at first.

"It isn't about what you want to do. This is our duty, and you will fulfill it!"

"I don't wanna! I don't wanna! I'm busy! Why don't you do it?!"

"Busy with what? Watching the telly? Coloring? You need to do some work around here!"

"But I'm a kid. It's my job to have dreams and unlimited potential. I am a god on earth."

"You will not call yourself a god!"

I didn't have many friends when I was little and would get picked on whenever I went into town. Thinking back on it, maybe my teacher thought giving me a job to do would give me purpose and a sense of belonging. And it was true; as I grew more used to the job, I began to perceive myself as a witch. It became my identity. I went from orphan to Lady Faust's apprentice, not just in my own mind but in the eyes of the townsfolk as well.

Had I never become a witch, I wonder if I ever would've found a place or purpose to call my own or, more likely, if I would've gotten stuck in my lack of identity. I probably would've let the fact that my parents had died before I could ever know them bring me down or lost hope over the fact that I had only one year left to live. Surely I would've wasted my final year doing nothing.

The reason I hadn't ended up like this was thanks to how busy I was back then. I was pretty much forced to take care of the woods, monitoring the dirt and planting herbs every day. The forest didn't look the same back then; the dirt was barren, and the distribution of magic was sporadic. Though there were trees, it was hard to call it a forest.

My mission was to bring this forest to life, and my greatest enemy was mint. All it took was one seed for this guy to take over a corner of my forest.

"Uw-waaah, *hic.* Those stupid mints keep killing my forest!!"

Unable to stop the onslaught of the mint menace, I came crying to my teacher.

"One mint too many and you've got a weed on your hands. I told you to be careful."

"The Witch's Forest is dead… We should burn it down and start from scratch, scorched-earth style."

"Enough, Meg. All things have their own lives, own characteristics, and own ways of life. You need to learn about your enemy and adapt to it. Witches must see the natural way of things in the world and live in harmony with it. Power isn't the key to fixing everything."

My teacher said this in an instructive tone. I felt like I could understand it now, though. Her words were not only the way of the witch but a guide by which I could live my life as well. I wasn't to get upset whenever something didn't go my way, but rather to make an effort to change myself for the better. This was what my teacher had likely meant.

As I put more work into the woods, it grew fuller with more trees, grass, and flowers. The soil grew richer and the expanse of forest wider. At some point, animals started populating the woods, and my teacher turned them into familiars. I tailored the forest into something the townsfolk could also enjoy, and it soon grew on the people of Lapis. Many of them would interact with their new animal neighbors, as well.

Looking back on it, my teacher had taught me how to take care of the soil, use magic, *and* live my life.

"Whew, this is great."

We returned to the manor, and I drew a hot footbath using mint oil to help wash Inori's feet. Every now and then, she'd grunt when I applied pressure to her feet as I massaged them.

"Mm, that's some soft skin you've got there, heugh-heugh-heugh."

"Cut it with the creepy voice."

Inori sighed deeply and looked up.

"This is heavenly, though. I can't remember the last time I've been able to relax like this."

"All that Sage stuff must really take its toll on you."

"It does. Working too much is like a poison. Actually, I think it's been a few days since I've had a bath."

"I'll whip one up for you after this, so please take one. I insist."

I'd better break out the strong soap for this one.

"Calm down. You'll go bald if you get upset over every little thing."

"Little...?"

The perplexity in my expression must've been obvious, because Inori smiled when she saw my reaction.

"You shouldn't laugh when you look at a lady's face."

"I like you. You should become my assistant once you've finished your training here."

"Your assistant?"

"In developing new medicine. We'd be partners. I work together with medical companies to find new substances with medicinal properties, test the effects, and verify their claims. We extract the substances from animals and plants, which involves breeding new species of plants, sometimes. I then use magic to amplify the effect of these substances. It's basically what you do here. I've actually been searching for someone well-versed in plants to become my assistant."

"This is all a bit sudden. I don't even know what my teacher would think..."

"That's why I said *when you're done here*. Think about it; there aren't many witches out there who've trained under *two* of the

Seven Sages. I bet you'd be all over the telly as an up-and-coming witch."

"You think I'd be on the telly...?"

My imagination ran wild. After I appeared on television, everyone would see how pretty I was, and I'd be an instant star. The people would find my personality entertaining, and I'd get on all the talk shows. From there, it was a television drama where I'd act alongside the main of the world's most popular boy band. We'd fall in love and get married, then live happily ever after in the penthouse suite of the city's tallest building.

"That could be fun..."

"Again, it's just something I want you to think about. If you're interested, I'll talk to Grandma Faust for you."

Inori spoke cheerfully, but I was very conflicted on the inside. I couldn't break it to her that I had less than a year to live.

"How old did you say you were?"

"Seventeen."

"So young. You're too clever for your age to be stuck in a small town like this. When I was in my teens, I was already traveling the world."

"You make yourself sound like a grandma when you talk about your younger years."

"You think I sound old...?"

Her comment made me think about how the thought of leaving this town, or this manor, for that matter, had never even crossed my mind before. The town of Lapis and the witch Faust's manor, living together with the townsfolk, my teacher, and our familiars—these were things I thought would never change.

"Traveling the world, eh...?"

When would I get the chance to do that? The most I can think about right now is the final year I have left to live.

"If you don't have any aspirations or ambitions for the future, sometimes traveling can help shed light on what's important to you."

"Aspirations and ambitions...like a goal?"

"Do you have one?"

Maybe before I was told I had a year left to live. Whatever I felt before that seemed more like a fleeting dream than anything now.

I took a brief moment to recall how I used to feel, then with a stern expression announced:

"World domination."

○

By the time I finished cleaning up after dinner, it was already well into the night. I quietly opened the front door.

"Come to me, White-Owl."

"Hoot."

White-Owl perched on my shoulder, and I sat on a stump in the garden to meditate. It was cold outside, but the night breeze felt good on my skin. The swaying of the grass and flowers in bloom in the Witch's Forest could be seen by the light of the moon. The only sound that could be heard that night was the chirping of crickets, and it was a full moon.

I used meditation to polish my spirit. With heightened focus, I did away with all that plagued my mind.

"Sure are a lot of bugs out here."

An unexpected voice from behind me cut through my intense focus. It was Inori.

"Are you meditating at night? Someone's stoic."

"It helps me focus. I have too many chores to do during the day, so night is the only time I get to myself."

"The night belongs to the witch, so maybe you're onto something."

"Want to join me, Inori?"

"I've never meditated before. They call me the Wise Witch for a reason, after all. My ideas and knowledge are enough for me to come up with magic on the spot. I'm a genius."

"Humble much?"

I looked up at the full moon. Seeing it high in the sky like that gave me a sense of excitement, like it was beckoning the witch blood that coursed through my veins. Although, whether there was an actual relationship between the moon and the blood of witches was beyond me.

"Inori. What would you do if you were told you only have a year left to live?"

This was meant to be a light question—some food for thought—but Inori's expression took on a serious look.

"What's that supposed to mean? Are you going to die?"

"I'm being hypothetical."

"No need to play games. I can tell what's happening."

With the glint of sadness in her eyes, she looked away.

"Do you think a girl your age can pull one over on the Wise Witch? I knew you were acting less animated whenever we talked about the future before."

"Heh-heh… You Seven Sages and your intuitions…"

Chuckling did nothing to lighten the mood.

"So why are you going to die?"

"I'm cursed."

"You're cursed?"

"It's called Death's Decree, and my teacher said that it will kill me. That once I turn eighteen, my biological clock will go berserk, and I'll start aging rapidly."

"Death's Decree…"

"Do you know about it?"

In utter silence, Inori shook her head.

"I didn't even realize you were cursed. There really is no telling when it comes to the higher-level curses, though."

"So it's safe to assume you don't know a way to dispel it?"

"This is the first time I've heard of such a curse. Curses are an ancient magic; I'm sure the only reason it was detectable was because of Grandma Faust… So what's her diagnosis?"

"She says there's less than a one percent chance I'll live. That I need to collect tears of joy from one thousand people."

"I see, you're going to make a seed of life. That would certainly put a stop to any curse that affects you through aging. But wow, talk about a tall order. How many tears have you collected so far?"

I removed the bottle attached to my belt and showed her.

"I have three tear shards. Only one of those is from joy, though."

"Well, that won't cut it."

"Yeah, I'm up shit creek without a paddle."

"Come on, now…"

"My teacher says the seed of life is made with tears of joy, which is why I'm collecting shards of emotion. Are these tiny rocks really that powerful?"

"Hard to say. I don't know too much about it."

"I thought you were supposed to be wise?!"

I was genuinely surprised.

"I am, but that doesn't mean I know everything. Especially something as niche as that."

"Niche…"

"Maybe *ancient* would be a better word for it. The magic of today doesn't work the same as it used to."

It wasn't just magic; the position of witches in society also varied greatly throughout the generations. The witches and wizards of the past used to perform miraculous acts of magic to protect the people and the land. Now, however, our magic was used more to promote and spread prosperity by supplementing research. Though it didn't mean all mages were researchers.

"Emotions aren't an element used in most modern spells. They are uncertain and difficult to re-create on demand. There isn't much use for a mage who can't cast spells when they are depressed, now, is there?"

"That's true."

Hearing Inori speak about this made it clear that even among witches, there were outlooks on magic that differed from my teacher's. My teacher focused more on ancient teachings, which placed more emphasis on human emotion, but Inori's style of magic was founded more in logic and science, an outlook closer to that of a scholar.

The way of magic did change throughout the generations. It felt like this difference between my teacher's and Inori's ways of thinking was a map of how magic had changed. There was a generational gap, or so it felt.

As this train of thought went chugging through my mind, it came to a sudden stop when Inori continued with "But...it has been maintained for a long time that tears have a strange power to them."

"Is that right?"

"I'm sure you've heard the old fairy tale about the mermaid who saved the prince with her tears, right? Tears of joy very well may have a sort of mysterious power to them that none of us know about, or an unknown power might exist within shards of emotion. It may sound like something out of a dream, but I enjoy those sorts of things."

"The older you get, the less room you have to dream, eh?"

"Don't make me hurt you."

As she said this, Inori must've realized something, because she averted her gaze from mine and stared right at the bottle in my hand.

"Do you mind if I take a look at your bottle?"

"Huh? Sure. I'll accept everything you own as collateral if you end up breaking it."

"I'll be careful."

Inori held up the bottle and squinted as she looked inside it.

"This might be my first time ever seeing a shard of emotion. I can sense a mysterious power to them."

"These are something a Sage hasn't seen before?"

"Of course. I've never tried to collect them."

That made sense. Most people would never have a reason to, and they weren't easy to come by even if you did—I could say that from experience.

"If you had to collect one thousand tears of joy, what would you do?"

"Hmm. Well, first I would test what qualifies as a tear of joy. I would need to run tests and collect data. Then I would produce a medicine or spell that could create the desired effect, find volunteers to test it on, and test it from there."

"Sounds mechanical."

"Such is the nature of an academic. However, I know it would be difficult. One year for one thousand tears… That's far tougher a trial than what I had to go through before finishing my apprenticeship."

"I can only imagine."

I stood up, and White-Owl hopped from my shoulder to my head. He flapped his wings and let out a soft hoot. His feathers shone in the moonlight, as if it was drawn to him.

"If I'm being honest with you, my heart danced when you invited me to work as your assistant. I've only ever lived in Lapis, so your offer felt like… How should I put this? A ticket to see the world. It excited me."

"Meg…"

"A few weeks have passed since my teacher had me start

collecting tears. I need to collect three a day, but here I am with a grand total of three. Positivity is my main personality trait, but it's not enough to keep me from acknowledging that one thousand tears in one year is pretty much impossible."

"While that may be true…isn't it a bit early for you to give up?"

"Give up…?"

She was right. I was trying to give up. What should've been obvious hit me all at once. I had stopped thinking about a year from now—stopped questioning my daily routine—and kept my mind occupied with other mundane thoughts. At some point, I settled with the fact that I was going to die instead of fighting to survive.

This realization shocked me, but a hearty chuckle from Inori snapped me out of my stupor.

"What's so funny? The weight of life and death on my shoulders?"

"Sorry, but I couldn't help but find it somewhat silly. How simple in the head must one be to fail to realize they've given up on life?"

"Those are fightin' words…"

"I'm sorry." Inori must've felt the prickle of my intense rage that I was sending her way. "Seeing as you no longer have the will to live, I'll show you something nice." Inori whipped her hair back with a single motion. "I'll show you why I'm a Sage."

○

"Did you know a meteor shower is supposed to pass by tonight?" Inori said while staring at the night sky.

"Is that so? Funny, there isn't a star in the sky tonight."

"That's because of the full moon. The meteors are passing over right now, but it is too bright to see them or any other stars. It isn't a good night for stargazing."

"That's a shame. I'd make a wish on one of them if I could see them."

"And what would someone who's forfeited life wish for?"

"Lots of money."

"You should really learn about at little thing called tact."

Inori couldn't hide her surprise as she let out a small sigh before extending her open hand toward the sky.

"Behold, the power of a Sage."

She then tightly clenched her fist.

It happened in the blink of an eye. Every star in the night sky could be seen clearly. The scale of a spell such as this would normally require multiple mages to chant a twelve-verse incantation around a giant magic circle, each channeling thorough knowledge of the physical world to cast their spell, but Inori managed to do all of this complicated groundwork with just the clench of her fist.

Hundreds of thousands, millions of stars burned brightly, lighting up the night sky that moments ago was lit only by the full moon. The Milky Way appeared across the heavens, sparkling against a backdrop of interstellar clouds in a dazzling array of colors.

"A sight like this is probably only visible from the edge of the earth."

"Whoa…"

"I'm not finished yet, though."

Inori etched out a character in the air.

"Come to me."

With this utterance, streaks of light began flying through the sky. It was the meteor shower. An impossible number of falling stars were raining down across the sky. As soon as one disappeared, another soon followed it, only to vanish once more. It was the visualization of a dream, or that's what it felt like. The

way the lights fell continuously really gave a new meaning to the word *meteor shower.*

"That sure is something… What did you do?"

"I changed the trajectory of the meteor shower a bit."

She said this like it was nothing.

"I bet it makes all those worries go away when you see the stars like this, doesn't it?"

"Yeah, I guess. I'll tell you once I find something to worry about."

"You can afford to worry a bit about the prospect of your life ending."

I'd given up. I'd given up and tried to accept the fact that I would die. I no longer even questioned why this was happening to me. *I guess I'm gonna die* was my outlook.

Seeing the meteor shower, though, made me realize something: The possibilities of magic were endless; that through the power of magic, miracles were possible, and the impossible was made possible; that there was always a way, no matter what.

These thoughts rushed through my mind as I watched the spectacle unfold. Maybe I could collect all the tears through one big show of magic that moved people far and wide, or maybe these tears weren't the only way for me to break the curse. I may end up even discovering another way to produce my own seed of life.

Magic carried with it an infinite number of results; the outcomes were as unlimited as magic itself.

"Make a wish, Meg. Wish for whatever you want most."

"Are you cheering on my campaign for world domination?"

"Let's choose a different wish." Inori brushed off my sarcasm with a stern gaze. "Wish to live. To not die. To become a witch who will step foot into the world. You should be wishing for things like this."

"Inori…"

I nodded quietly as she maintained her intense gaze.

"You're right."

Silently, I wished upon the stars. That I could live another year, and the year after that, and another ten years. That I could live to see the world. That the world I lived in would grow vast, and that I would live to see where it went. That one day, I would enter the world outside Lapis and meet even more people. That together with those new friends, I would create my own stories, stories that would amaze even my teacher.

This dream was the hope I needed to continue fighting.

"You know, I really do like you."

With a big smile on her face, Inori looked my way.

"I was confused at first. Why would Grandma Faust take on an apprentice?"

"She's always been pretty spontaneous."

Inori shook her head and grinned mischievously.

"Meg, you're gonna make a good witch one day."

While it didn't feel like an answer to Inori's confusion about my apprenticeship, it seemed she had no desire to shed further light on the matter. The real answer would likely keep me up at night.

○

My teacher returned two days later.

"Hello, I'm back."

Inori and I were met with shock when we walked into the foyer upon hearing her voice for the first time in what felt like ages.

"Look at you two! You shouldn't leave the kitchen with bread in your hands."

"A healthy mind requires a healthy body."

"Oh, hush."

"Teacher."

"Yes?"

"Welcome home."

"It's good to be back."

My teacher smiled before turning to face Inori.

"I apologize for thrusting this child upon you."

"It's fine. I actually had a lot of fun. How was the inspection?"

"There's a plant that was spreading rapidly due to an oversaturation of magic. It was the reason for the sudden change in the ecosystem. Luckily, there was still room for correction. I amended the damaged flow of magic in the soil, so the problem will resolve itself with time. Had we discovered this any later, the damage would've been irreparable."

"I'm glad you could fix it. I guess we can rest assured, for now."

"Yes. It was the biggest job I've been tasked with in a long while. Meg, my shoulders are killing me. Would you please rub them later?"

"You got it, Boss."

"Before that, Grandma Faust. There's something I wanted to ask you about."

"That's rare, coming from you. What is it?"

"Would you mind me taking in your apprentice as an assistant in the future?"

Inori wrapped her arms around my neck in a headlock-like pose as she said this. My teacher was thrown off by the sudden request.

"I've taken quite the liking to her. She knows her stuff about magic. You sure have raised a good mage."

"She still has a ways to go; there's still a lot she must learn."

She followed this with "But...when the time comes, I suppose that could be a good option for her."

"Then it's settled!"

Inori happily snapped her fingers.

"You heard her, Meg! So don't go dying on me, okay? You're gonna be my right-hand witch, so live even if it kills ya."

"That doesn't make any sense."

"Ah, ah, ah. No smart talk. I just need an answer."

The rigidity of her stern gaze as she stared straight into my eyes suggested she wasn't going to entertain any ifs, ands, or buts. Her eyes twinkled with the spark of a child about to embark on a grand adventure—an adventure I was evidently going to be a part of, as the infectious twinkle soon spread to me.

"You got it. I'll stay alive. How else will I become a witch who walks alongside you and my teacher at the top of the world?"

"That's the spirit! I'm glad positivity is your only personality trait!"

"It's not my *only* one."

"I was just repeating what you said earlier."

"Look at you two; you're like sisters."

Watching the two of us jest with each other put a smile on my teacher's face.

"Great. Now that Grandma Faust is back, how about we get back to eating breakfast?"

"That sounds nice. Meg, please prepare some toast and tea for me."

"Sure thing. Hey, Teacher."

"What is it?"

"What was the reason you took me in as an apprentice anyway?"

This question caught my teacher off guard, but shaking off the surprise, she responded:

"Who knows?"

That was all she had to say about the topic, and it looked like my sleepless nights would continue for the time being as I pondered the answer to this question.

The Wise Witch gave me my dream. A dream, which awaited me at the end of this year after having survived my curse, to live on in a world of countless possibilities and experience the whole wide world outside Lapis. This dream rekindled my desire to live—I needed to live if I was going to see it through.

"Meg! What are you doing! Hurry up and put the kettle on!"

"Yeah, yeah! I'll get right to it!"

Which is why—for now, at least—I need to focus on the task at hand, no matter how small, while I live for the dream that awaits.

Chapter 4:
Those
Shrouded
by Death

From a very young age, it wasn't uncommon for me to witness strange things.

"Hey! Teacher!"
"What is it, Meg?"
"Why is that person all dark?"
There was a man shrouded in a dark, black mist. He was strangely transparent, like he was going to disappear at any minute.
Hearing me say this, my teacher patted me on the head.
"So you can see him?"
She said this with a sad tone.

That younger version of me soon learned that those wreathed in such mist were those who had passed.

The black mist also came to those soon to die—most of the time with only a month left to live. My teacher called the mist Death, like the grim reaper.
"I thought Death wore a suit?"
"Why would it wear a suit? What kind of shows have you been watching…?"
"It was actually a movie."
"That isn't the point!"
At the time, I was consuming movies like a kid in a candy store, which gave me a false idea of what Death would look like.

* * *

The black mist didn't always appear, but at the same time, there were also people who were covered in a particularly thick mist.

Whether it be old age, late-stage cancer, or a grave wound that couldn't be patched up, a thick haze appeared around those who could not escape their fate.

Ten years have passed since I first saw the mist. Even now, I occasionally see Death.

○

"Dr. Hendyyy! I've got this week's order of coolants and medicine-enhancing herbs for you."

"Oh, thank you, Meg. You can place the box right there."

"You got it, Boss."

I was making a medicinal herb delivery to Dr. Hendy and the other doctors in town. Providing herbal brews and other witch services was a part of my apprenticeship.

As I unloaded a couple of marked boxes from my cart, I heard a young voice exclaim, "Ah!" from behind me.

"It's the friendly neighborhood witch!"

"Ah! It's the friendly neighborhood Anna! Hello there."

"Let's go play!"

"Sorry, but I'm on the clock."

"Aw, not even for a few minutes? Don't act like some dumb grown-up."

"Ha-ha-ha. Call me what you will, but I'll have you know, I'm one busy witch, little Anna."

"You're ugly."

"Who're you callin' ugly, twerp?! You want a knuckle sandwich?!"

"Whoops! I made her angry!"

I was teasingly chasing a giggling Anna around the doctor's office waiting room when we both heard a hearty chuckle come from the corner of the room. The feminine voice had a gentle tone, one that was warm and calmed whoever heard it.

"When did you two become such close friends?"

It was Grandma Flaire, an old woman who lived just outside town. She'd been sitting in one of the chairs in the waiting room. Her house, where she lived alone, had the most beautiful garden. She was a nice woman; I'd never seen her angry before. When I was younger, she'd taught me how to grow flowers, but this was the first time I'd seen her in a long time.

"Flaire! You look so old. It's been a while. It's a shame we had to meet again in a stuffy old doctor's office."

"Is it really that stuffy in here...?"

Dr. Hendy sounded sad from behind the reception desk.

"You sure have grown, Meg. It's good to see you doing well. And Carbuncle, too."

With a "*Squeak*," Carbuncle emerged from one of the boxes.

When did he get in there?

"You little trickster. Did you tag along again? You're supposed to be watching the manor with White-Owl."

"*Squeak...*"

"Oh, please forgive him. I know how fond he is of you."

"He's such a little ball of energy. I wonder who he gets that from?"

"He's just like you."

"Stay outta this, kid."

As we shared this exchange, my eyes wandered to the paper bag Grandma Flaire was carrying. It bore a prescription for a medicine with a familiar name.

"Hey, I made that magical medicine."

"That's right. I take it with the medicine for my joint pain. It really helps; you're the only reason I can walk at all nowadays."

"I'm glad to hear it. You're going to be eighty this year, right? Please take care of yourself."

"Heh-heh, hearing that from a youngin' like you gives me all the energy I need."

"Are you going home after this?"

"No, I am going to take a walk through some woods outside of town. There is a sacred tree out there, and a big one at that."

I stood and helped Grandma Flaire to her feet from her chair.

"I'll be on my way, Dr. Hendy. Thank you for everything. I'll be seeing you, too, little Anna."

"Have a nice day."

"Bye-bye, Granny."

"Thank you for your help, too, Meg. I'll be fine on my own."

"You sure? Be careful. You know what—do you mind if I come and visit soon? I want you to teach me more about your flower garden."

"Of course. Feel free to visit whenever you please."

With an "I'll see you then," I waved to Grandma Flaire from the doctor's office door.

That was when, just for a flash, I saw it. A familiar black mist clinging to Grandma Flaire.

Goose bumps spread across my entire body, and I audibly gulped. The sight made me feel nauseous, and my body began to tremble. Even though it was cold that day, I could feel sweat dripping down my forehead.

"What's wrong, Meg?"

Anna could tell something was bothering me. Seeing the concerned look on her face brought me out of my shock, and then I noticed Dr. Hendy walking toward me.

"Are you all right, Meg? You seem pale. If you're not feeling well, you..."

"No, I'm fine. I never get sick."

"Are you sure? It's cold season right now, so be careful."

"Thanks. By the way, is Grandma Flaire ill with something serious?"

"No, I don't think so. Why?"

"Oh, it's nothing."

Death had latched on to Grandma Flaire. It was heaven's way of saying her time would soon be up.

○

Grandma Flaire was going to die—and soon. While it wasn't set in stone, the mist was never wrong before. All who were shrouded in it perished. Even after I left Dr. Hendy's office, it was all I could think about.

"Meg… Meg! Meg Raspberry!"

"Huh?"

Hearing my name brought me back to reality. I was sitting at the kitchen table with a plate of spaghetti in front of me, and my teacher was looking at me.

"Stop spacing out and finish your meal."

"Sorry."

I watched as my teacher sighed before focusing on her dinner.

"Teacher…"

"What is it?"

"Is there a way to save someone who has Death clinging to them?"

My teacher's fork froze in midair as I said this.

"Did you see the mist today?"

I didn't say anything, though my teacher could likely see right through my silence. I was too afraid to say Grandma Flaire's name out loud.

"You've seen it before, and you know what happens to those followed by the black mist. There's nothing we can do to help them."

Her words pierced right through my heart. The Eternal Witch continued, as if to enlighten me.

"Fate exists, and Death merely follows the rules of fate. You who can see the mist should understand this more than others."

"What about a seed of life? Couldn't I use one to stop it?"

"Meg."

My teacher whispered the next part.

"Fate is not something that should be bent."

There was a gentleness to her expression and a weight behind her words as well.

"You're the one who always says a witch needs to live with the way of the world. Wouldn't that mean using a seed of life on myself would effectively be bending my own fate?"

"There are fates in this world that can be tampered with and those that we must not."

"Whose right is it to decide that?!"

Without really thinking, I slammed my fists on the table and stood up. The sudden noise must've shocked my teacher's nearby familiars, because they all jumped. I was breathing heavily—my voice was quivering; I could barely control my emotions. The tension was less than ideal for a plate of pasta.

"Meg, you need to calm down."

"I won't! I refuse to!"

Despite my lack of composure, my teacher remained calm.

"A witch's role is to recognize the natural way of things in the world and live in harmony with it. We may tamper with fate for those who wish to live on, but it isn't right to force someone who doesn't wish it to live beyond their time. You would only be changing their fate for yourself, which you mustn't. It isn't wrong to save a life, but does the life you wish to save truly want that?"

My teacher had a sad look in her eyes.

"Do not avert your gaze from the reality of things. It isn't right to extend one's life just because you want to. Do not...make the same mistake as me."

It was rare for my teacher to say something so personal. She didn't want me to make the same mistake as her. I could tell my teacher carried something painful from her past with her, something she probably had never told me about.

"When met with someone whose death is upon them, it is our job to see that they can leave this would peacefully, with no regrets."

"Our job..."

"Meg. Your ability to see Spirits and Death and the powerful magic in your eyes are unique to you. These are things that mages can't attain even after years and years of hard work. You have a power they can only dream of having—and you have it for a reason, Meg Raspberry. Your powers have a purpose."

"A purpose?"

"Don't you suppose there is something you and only you can do for those soon to be visited by Death? A way you can help them spend their limited, precious time left in this world?"

"I think saving them from Death is something I could do."

"Meg...!"

"So what, we're not allowed to save people just because they aren't necessarily asking for it? Then why do doctors save people who tried to end their own lives?! Your point of view on this is too one-sided!"

"That isn't what I mean! I'm simply telling you that you mustn't misinterpret the reality of things!"

"So?! What's wrong with saving someone we may have the power to save?! I just want to save someone I see in need. That's the reality of this conversation!"

My breathing was heavy and irregular.

"Who knows when that dark mist will start hovering around me? Are you going to tell me to give up on making my seed of life when that happens, too...?"

It was evident that my teacher had no response to this remark. I picked up the half-eaten plate in front of me and dumped it altogether into the sink.

"I can't sit by and let someone I might be able to save die, nor do I want to. What you call *the way of the world* isn't something I want to take part in if it means watching people die."

"Meg!"

As I stormed out of the room, my thudding stomps almost drowned out my teacher's voice as she called my name. Grandma Flaire was always there for us... A soft-spoken, gentle woman, she loved her flowers, and I wanted her to live a peaceful life. So if there was even the smallest chance that I could do something for her, I certainly wasn't going to give up on it.

I'm going to do something. It isn't like me...to hesitate like this. I've always acted before thinking; why change now? Grandma Flaire may not have much time left, but I want to do what I can with the time she still has. Or else I'll spend what's left of my own life in regret.

"C'mon, boys! We're gonna take action!"

Making straight for the front door, I shouted this, and my two trusty familiars—Carbuncle and White-Owl—joined me as I reached for the doorknob.

"Meg."

I heard my teacher call out to me with a firm voice. Her expression was one of understanding, as if she'd come to a new realization... She stared with sadness in her gaze.

"Whatever happens, you must accept the outcome. The greater the effort you put forward, the greater the pain will be... for you."

"We can't know that until I try...!"
I opened the door and ran off into the dark night.

○

"Oh, if it isn't Meg. I never expected a visit at this hour."
Grandma Flaire opened the door. She was visibly shocked by the sight of me smiling at her with a suitcase in my hands.
"Heh, I got into a fight with my teacher and, you know, kind of ran away from home."
Though there was a smile on my face, the cold was nothing to be smiling about. It wasn't quite winter yet, but autumn was coming close to its end, and the nights were very cold. Grandma Flaire could see my teeth chattering, and she said, "Oh my," before ushering me in. "It's freezing outside. Please come in."
"Yeah, thank you."
Running away probably wasn't my best display of good judgment, but there's no point in lamenting over it now that I'm here. And life is supposed to be a journey, right?!
"Whew, it's cold out there."
The fireplace crackled as I warmed my hands over it. Most modern homes used hydrothermal heating systems, but older ones still used fireplaces. Grandma Flaire had lived in this home for who knew how many years, so it made sense that she still heated her home the old-fashioned way. I preferred this method, seeing as the manor also relied on a fireplace for warmth.
My two familiars were huddled up next to me, and the flickering of the flame could be seen in the reflections of their big eyes. The way they stayed close to me always served to remind me that they were my familiars.
"This is the first time in years you've fought with Lady Faust like this, isn't it? What happened?"
"It's so dumb, it isn't even worth talking about. My teacher got

angry at me for trying to cook one of the yummier-looking familiars, so I defended myself using Buddhist karmic principles, only for my teacher to go off on how religious differences can often spark war, but I retorted that all beings are fundamentally the same—predestined to become stardust in the vast void. It's all so...pointless, you know? Everything's just a chaotic, indifferent jumble. But hey, this might be old news to you."

Grandma Flaire murmured her reply. "That sounds very difficult." It was clear she had no idea what I was talking about. At the same time, I could also tell she seemed happy.

"Are you smiling?"

"Oh, excuse me. I just remembered how my husband and I used to get into arguments all of the time."

"You? Getting into fights? Now, *that's* hard to believe."

"When you live together with someone long enough, you'll get into a fight or two eventually. It's the best way to learn about someone else, though, little by little."

With a thin smile, Grandma Flaire turned her gaze to a picture on the wall. It was her late husband and their son, who had moved far away from Lapis. Grandma Flaire had been living alone in this home for a long time.

What must it feel like to live in such a big house all alone?

"Hey, Grandma Flaire. Do you mind if I stay here with you for a little while? I don't think I can face my teacher yet."

"That's fine by me, but won't Lady Faust be worried?"

"That's fine. She has an All-Seeing Eye if she wants to check in on me. She already knows where I am and probably even when I'll go back. And I've been meaning to catch up with you anyway."

"In that case...feel free to make yourself at home."

She said this with a warm smile, her eyes squinting as she did. Seeing her smile like this made it worth the trip.

"Have you already eaten? You must be hungry."

"Oh, no. Don't worry about—"

I tried to politely decline the offer but was cut off by a loud growling sound. I immediately sprang up in shock—thinking a bear was trying to get into the house—but was even more shocked when I realized it was my own stomach rumbling!

Thinking back on it, I'd stormed out after throwing away my largely untouched dinner.

Hey, a girl's gotta eat.

"Heh-heh. Wait here, I have some delicious stew on the stove."

Grandma Flaire turned on her stove and heated up a premade stew. It didn't take long for its alluring smell to fill the room, and shortly after, she placed a bowl of stew on the table. Judging by its color, it seemed to use red wine as its base—and that just amplified my appetite. Enthralled by the presentation, I took my seat before taking a bite of the stew. It was piping hot—I let out little puffs of breath to cool it as I ate—and had a rich taste.

"The cold brings it all: fights, sadness, and difficulties. Almost like it chills the heart. What a chilled heart needs is some nice warm food. It's funny; a warm meal can mellow you out, help strike up a conversation, and before you know it, even do away with ill will."

"Do away with ill will, you say…"

Being together with Grandma Flaire gave me that feeling. She was such a warm person that it made me feel warm on the inside as well.

I wish she could always be here, forever.

With this on my mind, I enjoyed the stew she'd prepared for me.

○

I sidled into Grandma Flaire's bed together with her. I'd told her I was all right taking the couch, but she insisted that sleeping in the same bed would keep us nice and toasty. Carbuncle even helped himself to some space on our sheets, which served to crowd the bed even more.

I don't want to hear any fuss if we end up smooshing you.

White-Owl perched on the windowsill, where he hooted like the owl he was. His hoots always let me know the day was over.

"Meg? What are you doing?"

"It gets cold at night once you put the fire out, right? I'm going to use some magic to help keep the current temperature throughout the night."

"Wow, I didn't know you could do that."

I dropped some magical herbs into the fireplace before chanting a twelve-part incantation. With that, the burning herbs quickly disintegrated into a haze, which dissipated throughout the room. This would prevent the room from being affected by the temperatures outdoors.

"It's been so long since I last stayed here with you."

"Yes, I recall you were still a small child the last time you did. You had fought with Lady Faust that day, too."

I'd run away from home before when I was a little kid, much like I had today.

"Meg, it's your responsibility to take care of the forest. What are you doing wandering around here?"

"Shut up, shut up, shut uuup! Why am I! The only one! Who has to work! All the time?! Why don't *you* watch the forest if you love it so much?!"

"Your behavior is ludicrous! Do not avert your eyes from your own laziness! You have to earn your meals around here!"

"Then I'll fast like a monk and maybe achieve enlightenment while I'm at it! You're so mean! I hope you get reincarnated as something bad!"

"Come now, Meg! Where are you going?! Meg!"

I'd left the manor and wandered through Lapis. I didn't have anywhere to go, but it would feel like I'd lost if I went home. I was looking up at the sky listlessly, when…

"Oh my. Are you all right, little one?"

…Grandma Flaire found me. She took me in and gave me some stew. From that day on, I would go to her house, where she would teach me about flowers and gardening. Despite this being so long ago, I could still remember the time we spent together like it was yesterday. This was likely because Grandma Flaire was still the same person she used to be.

"Your bed smells like flowers, just like you."

"Is that so? I was taking care of my flowers today, so maybe some of their fragrance rubbed off on me."

The scent was calming in a nostalgic sort of way. I took a deep breath before turning onto my back and facing her ceiling. It was a ceiling I knew well, though it was old and beginning to wear. This was likely because this house, which was meant for a family, was simply too large for a single elderly woman to maintain.

"Your house is getting a bit old, isn't it? It's been…how many years since your son left to live on his own?"

"I can't even remember. It's been so many years since he left."

"Have you seen him lately?"

"He used to come and see me at the end of every year, but he hasn't been able to lately since he's become so busy."

"I see…"

The loud ticking of her wall clock struck my ears. I didn't know what to do; was it better for me to tell her that she might die soon? That it may be a good idea for her to visit her son again soon? I'd come here with the intent to save her from that death, but nothing was set in stone. Even if I taught her about the seed of life, there was a greater chance of Death taking her before we could ever create one. With there being no real plan B, the last thing I wanted was for my friend to leave this life with regret.

I couldn't say it, though, not when I saw her smiling face. It made me realize how scary it was to tell someone about their death. Once a person knew, there was no going back to the bliss of ignorance.

"You're going to die, Meg. It'll happen in a year."

Hearing that had changed my fate forever. I could only wonder how much courage my teacher had needed to muster up to tell me.

"Is something the matter, Meg?"

Grandma Flaire was looking at me with an affectionate expression.

"It looks like you have something on your mind."

"Oh, you know, it's just, uh…witch things…"

Unable to make up my mind about it yet, I tried to shrug off her concern for me, but she responded with "I see. I don't know much about magic, but I'm always here if you need someone to listen." Grandma Flaire then smiled before continuing. "It always warms my heart to see you smiling, Meg."

"Grandma Flaire…"

What should I do? What is it that I can do? What can I do for my friend? How much longer does she have…?

With all the questions on my mind, I couldn't calm down. Was it right to live your final days knowing you may die? Or was it better to live them happily? I couldn't figure out which was right.

○

"They're growing well this year."

We were in Grandma Flaire's garden. It was elevated, with a brick border, and had a variety of different plants sprouting in it. Though it was cold, there were many flowers that blossomed at this time of year. Blooming pansies, violas, and Christmas cactuses lined one part of the garden, with the herbs being planted in a different spot. It was quite a feat for this variety of plants to coexist in the same garden without impeding one another, a testament to Grandma Flaire's meticulous effort in pruning them and keeping the dirt healthy.

"If you see something you like, feel free to take it home with you. I harvest many seeds every year."

"Hmm, perhaps a new face could bring life to my empire..."

Three days passed. I found time to go to the library and study magic here and there, but there wasn't much information on Death, let alone a method to save my friend. The time we spent together was relatively mundane, but there was a warm comfort to it. Something about it felt like it would last forever.

"Oh my, look at the time. Would you like to join me for a walk, Meg?"

"It is a nice time for a walk."

It was two in the afternoon. The only people who could go for a walk at this time were university students set to graduate with a job already lined up, the unemployed, and old people. Which did I fall under? I was a witch, which definitely wasn't unemployed.

"It looks like you go on walks every day. Don't you ever get tired of them?"

"I like to observe the growth of the plants and how the town changes every day; it has a strange way of keeping me happy and healthy. I'm sure the only reason I can walk at all at this age is thanks to this habit."

"You might be onto something there."

I learned quickly that Grandma Flaire liked to walk to new places every day. Today, we were headed somewhere different from the day before. Judging by the direction, it looked like we were going to the park north of town.

It was a bright and sunny day, and the marketplace was bustling with busy mothers buying food for their families. Carbuncle ran around us at my feet, with White-Owl occasionally picking him up for the pair to glide around for fun. I walked slowly next to Grandma Flaire, matching her footsteps with my own.

With every step she took, it felt to me like she was walking closer to her impending death. She would walk, slowly but surely, until she couldn't anymore. I shook my head to stop myself from thinking such thoughts.

"Maybe we should take a little break."

Grandma Flaire moved toward a bench near the entrance of the park as she said this, and I decided it would be best to try and keep any intrusive thoughts out of my mind. I sat down next to her, and she took something out of her bag that was wrapped in paper and smelled really nice.

"What is that delicious smell?"

"They're biscuits. I woke up early to make them while you were asleep."

"Talk about the royal treatment! You make me feel like a princess..."

They were herb biscuits. I took a bite, and the crunchy sweetness filled my palate and then was followed by a hint of rosemary. I didn't know how long it'd been since I had Grandma Flaire's homemade cookies. I was almost trembling with delight as I savored the flavor, and then Grandma Flaire produced a steaming cup of warm tea.

"You can't have biscuits without tea, now, can you?"

"You must be a goddess, because this is heaven..."

The fragrant tea soothed my body and soul.

I feel at peace. It almost makes everything—Grandma Flaire's situation, my curse, and my fight with my teacher—seem like it never even happened.

I knew this was just my mind running away from the problem, but it really did feel like that after the past three days of being so stressed about everything.

I was so preoccupied with trying to find an answer that it was likely starting to take a toll on my mental health.

"So, Grandma Flaire, where are we headed—?"

Turning to look at her while I spoke, I stopped mid-sentence in utter shock.

I could see the darkness.

No, this isn't the black mist... It is Death itself.

The thickness of the mist was unlike anything I'd ever seen before, and it was enveloping Grandma Flaire.

"Grandma Flaire!"

The mist dissipated with my shout, allowing me to see Grandma Flaire's friendly face once more. She seemed like her usual self, so I sighed with relief.

"Oh, I must've dozed off. I often do that on nice warm days like this. Is there something wrong, Meg? You don't look so well."

"I'm perfectly fine! The world could end tomorrow, and I'd be crawling around on the ground alive with the cockroaches. What about you, though, Grandma Flaire? How's your health been?"

"That's a bit of a sudden question, but I suppose I've been getting more tired recently. Especially on nice days like this. It is almost as if the sun's warmth lulls me to sleep. It feels so nice, doesn't it?"

"Yeah..."

Her sleepiness was trying to invite her to an eternal slumber, or so it felt. Seeing the thick black smog kicked the rose-colored glasses right off my face and brought me back to reality. It was Grandma Flaire who stood up and said, "Let's get a move on, shall we?" while I worried over what I'd just seen.

"I want to show you a very special place to me."

"Okay… I look forward to it."

Grandma Flaire led me to the woods at the far end of the park, where the town's largest tree stood.

"This is it."

"So this is your special spot."

"That's right. This tree is a god that protects our town."

Grandma Flaire looked up at the tall tree with a smile on her face. I had come to this tree a few times before. Every year when it began to get warmer outside, countless flowers bloomed around this tree. This was because of the magic that flowed from its roots into the ground; the tree shared its magic with the surrounding plants. Thanks to this, the park had some of the prettiest flower gardens in all of Lapis during that time of year.

To call the tree a god that protects the town wasn't entirely inaccurate.

"I've visited this place often ever since I was a little girl. I played with my friends here, spent afternoons with my family under it, and now, I've been able to bring you here, too. This tree has continuously watched over me."

Grandma Flaire walked up to the tree and placed her hand on its trunk; she spoke about the tree as if it was an old friend.

"So you've always been together."

"That's right, ever since I was young."

I stood next to Grandma Flaire and placed my hand on the tree trunk.

"Oh…"

"Is there something wrong?"

"No, it's nothing."

The tree's flow of magic was a bit messy. It was also absorbing much more magic from the earth than normal. At this rate, it wouldn't take long for the tree to be negatively impacted. It would either overflow with magic and begin to wither or would be cut down before it brought down the rest of the ecosystem with it. Perhaps thanks to how often I came into contact with plants, I could already tell that there was no saving this tree.

It was almost like I could tell the tree's fate.

"Fate exists, and Death merely follows the rules of fate......... That isn't what I mean! I'm simply telling you that you mustn't misinterpret the reality of things!"

Oh, I get it now.

Everything my teacher said made sense to me, all at once.

What was happening to the tree was also happening to Grandma Flaire—there was no saving them. There were fates that could and could not be changed, and Grandma Flaire...was the latter.

It was the way the world worked—God's way. All life came to an end.

This was what it meant to be shrouded in the black mist—to be visited by Death.

It was now clear to me why I'd come here. I knew what I, someone with less than a year left to live, needed to do after learning about Grandma Flaire's death.

"Grandma Flaire."

"Yes?"

"What if, say, the world was to end tomorrow? What would you want to do before you die?"

"That's a big question. But yes, I suppose I'd like to spend my final day with my family."

"You don't say..."

I looked up into the sky. Faced with someone whose death was nearing them, it was our job to see to it that their final moments with us were spent in a way they wouldn't regret.

It was our duty.

○

The next morning came.

I woke up before the sun came out and carefully got out of bed so as to not wake up Grandma Flaire. Waking up this early was part of my daily routine anyway. I got dressed and went outside, where I was embraced by the frigid early morning air. White puffs of breath escaped my mouth, and with every breath I took, I could feel the chilly air enter my lungs.

"Hoot."

"Good morning to you, too."

Perched on the mailbox outside was White-Owl. He'd been waiting for me with his big round eyes. I gave him a nod. We would leave Carbuncle behind this time, as he was sleeping in bed with Grandma Flaire.

"Let's go."

"Hoot."

I extended my arm for White-Owl, who flew over and took perch, and then gently rubbed his head, causing him to shut his eyes with delight.

I then began my twelve-part incantation.

"My loyal kin—heed my call—dance far and wide, in the vast sky's hall—release your inner power—my wish stretches beyond what eyes can pin—grant me a way to a distant land—as a messenger that flies with wings so grand—slice through

the heavens—the clouds around you will bend—carry the wind—along with my life—"

I swung my arm wide, and White-Owl took flight. I followed behind, running forward and planting one foot on the wall in front of the house. Without losing any momentum, I then leaped up into the sky.

"—and ascend!"

I was mid-jump when *something big* caught me and whisked me up and away. The earth below grew distant, and wind blew my hair in every direction. The air was cold against my cheeks and fingers at this height, but I soon found feathery warmth on the back of the giant owl who carefully carried me as we flew up higher and higher.

Witches had a special relationship with their familiars. It was possible for the creatures to become the catalysts for their master's magic. The spell I'd cast on White-Owl made him grow almost ten times his original size.

"Okay! Off to the capital!"

"Hoot!"

I knew exactly where we needed to go. I'd looked it up the night before. Grandma Flaire had a letter with the address on it. I was sure the person I needed to find would be there. White-Owl soared through the sky, cutting through the clouds, headed straight for London.

It was still early enough in the morning for the roads to be empty. Everything was quiet, and the air was brisk. I stood before a lone brick building. It was a large house with a red roof and beautiful decorations.

I knocked on the window, and after a brief wait, a young girl emerged from behind the curtain on the inside. She seemed to be twelve or thirteen, as far as I could tell.

Our eyes met, and I smiled and waved at her. Her eyes widened with surprise in return.

"Whoa… That's amazing!"

It made sense that she would be surprised to see me, seeing as this was the second floor and I was riding on top of an owl that was taller than their house.

"Hello, young lady."

"Who are you?"

"I'm a witch. A friend of your grandmother's. Is your dad at home?"

"Yeah, but I think he's still sleeping. Are you here to see him?"

"I am. Do you think you could go get him for me?"

"Okay. Dad! There's a witch here to see you!"

The young girl ran inside, and before long, a sleepy-looking husband and wife came back with her. It was Grandma Flaire's son, Ed, and his wife. He looked at me from the open window, braving the cold air blowing in, before speaking up.

"Oh, I know you… You're Lady Faust's apprentice…"

"Meg Raspberry. I know it's been a while since we've seen each other, but I'm going to need you to take the day off from work today."

"Huh?"

I gave a soft smile to Ed's confused daughter.

"I said, take off from work."

○

It didn't take long for Carbuncle to realize his master was away.

"Squeak?"

He called out for her. White-Owl wasn't there, either.
"*Squeak, squeak...*"
"Oh my. Is something wrong, little one?"
The noise he made as he searched for his master woke up Grandma Flaire, too. She gave the lonely familiar a gentle hug to calm him down.
"That's odd. Wherever could she be?"
The two searched the house. They checked the bathroom; I wasn't in the tub, the toilet, nor the sink.
Their search was interrupted by a loud *thud* from outside. The two looked at each other before making their way to the foyer and opening the front door. The cold air rushed in, wrapping around them both.
"Oh, it sure is cold today."
"*Squeak...*"
The two scanned the front yard for Meg; puffs of white filled the air as they turned their heads. It wouldn't take long for them, however, to notice the flapping noise coming from somewhere. It was a bit strange; the flapping was much heavier than any bird she'd heard before.
"Grandma Flaaaaire!"
"Meg...?"
The pair looked up, and their breath caught. It was White-Owl, with me and three other passengers on board.
"Guess who's here to see you!"
I motioned with my hand, and Grandma Flaire's granddaughter, Lily, poked her happy little head out of White-Owl's feathers. "Hello, Grandmother!"
From under the group, Grandma Flaire and Carbuncle stared wide-eyed.
"C'mon, you guys! Ed and the missus!"
"Ah, ha-ha... Hey, Mum."

"I-it is good to see you again, Flaire."

Seeing her son's family waving from atop a giant owl, Grandma Flaire called back cheerfully, "Welcome home."

"You really surprised us, showing up out of nowhere this morning. You made it sound like my mother was unwell."

The sun was up over the park by then. Ed and I sat on the same bench I'd sat on the other day. I watched his wife and daughter play, but I could feel his eyes like darts on my skin as he said this.

"You're the one who never comes home anymore. I was just giving you a chance to."

"That's easy for you to say. Ugh… I had a really important meeting planned for today."

"What's more important, seeing your mother for the first time in years or going to some meeting?"

"Those are two very different things!"

Ed and I shared some prickly back-and-forth, only to be quelled by his mother. "Now, now." She had hot tea ready in a thermos. "You know Meg meant no harm by it. And she's right; you haven't been able to take time off in years. You should enjoy the opportunity."

"Listen, I…"

Ed's expression up until that point made it clear he was upset over the situation, but as soon as he took a sip of tea, he said, "I don't know how long it's been since I've come to this spot."

"Feeling a bit nostalgic?"

"I used to play here all the time when I was a kid, with my dad before he passed away. You know that one giant tree in the woods? We used to go and see it together. We'd play all morning, then Mum would give us biscuits and lunch."

"That was so much fun."

Grandma Flaire smiled like she was watching the sight her son described unfold before her. She'd called this place her favorite spot. It was clear that it was full of memories for her.

"Dad! Come over here!"

Lily waved her hand for her dad, who, with a "Here we go," stood up.

"I've been summoned."

"Go have some fun."

Ed walked toward his daughter and wife, leaving me and Grandma Flaire behind watching him. The two of us shared a small chuckle.

"Lily sure has gotten big."

"When was the last time you got to see her?"

"Back when she was three or four. To be honest, I half expected her to have forgotten about me."

"Looks like she's got a good memory on her. This one's got a bright future, eh?"

We were watching the family of three play joyfully together on the green grass when Grandma Flaire turned to me and quietly said, "Thank you, Meg. You could tell that I missed them, couldn't you?"

"I remember every night you let me stay with you and every meal and cookie you shared with me. I just hope this wasn't all a bother."

"Don't worry about that. This has made me so happy."

"I'm glad to hear it."

Grandma Flaire had a nice big smile on her face. Seeing her this happy took some of the weight off my heavy heart.

"Meg, I just know that you'll be the world's best witch one day."

"You really think so?"

"I'm certain of it. You have my word."

"Well, your word means the world to me."

I smiled, and Grandma Flaire continued to look at me with her friendly gaze.

"I'm so glad we met, Meg."

"Well, that came from nowhere, didn't it?"

"I've lived a long life, and I've met more than my fair share of witches. But it was you who gave me the most, Meg. I can tell you have the ability to fill the holes in the hearts of those close to you… That's the kind of witch you are."

"That's a bit of a stretch."

"It really isn't. It was you and you alone who let me spend such a wonderful day like this with my beloved family. To be together with them, and with you, is more than I could ever ask for."

Her eyes grew teary, and with a smile, she looked out at the park—at the world.

"To think I could see something so beautiful this late in my life…"

"What are ya talkin' about? This is barely scratching the surface. Once I'm a real witch, I'll be able to show you much, much more."

"Will you?"

"For sure. Right now, one of the Seven Sages wants me to become her assistant. Once I graduate from my teacher's tutelage, I'll see the world. I'll get all the training I need there and be able to use even more incredible magic."

"Wow, that does sound nice…"

"Her name is Inori, and she's a witch from the East. She knows everything there is to know about plants. Actually, when she first came to visit us at the manor…I don't know if it was because she was busy with the conference or what, but her feet reeked, and—"

That's when it happened—a *clink*.

What was that?

Strangely enough, I felt it on my waist. I took out the bottle, and lo and behold; it was a tear of joy. But whose?

"Is this…?"

I looked over at Grandma Flaire. She had her eyes closed as

she quietly basked in the warm sun. She looked so peaceful, almost like she was sleeping.

"Grandma Flaire? Did you fall sleep?"

She didn't respond. Her eyes remained closed, as peacefully as could be.

"Granny?"

Then it hit me.

My breathing became unsteady, and I couldn't speak. My trembling increased, little by little. I couldn't think straight, and then—

"She's asleep and at peace."

It was the Eternal Witch. She was standing in front of me with a sincerely affectionate, sad look on her face as she said this.

"To be at such peace when she fell into her final sleep meant that she was truly happy."

"Teacher…"

"To change the end, Meg, isn't something anyone can do. You, however, learned of hers, and you acted. For her sake and her sake alone. Thanks to you, Mrs. Flaire was able to spend her final moments with her precious family. Though it isn't possible to change the outcome, you can change its manifestation…just like you did today."

My teacher then gently embraced me.

"You did well, Meg…"

My teacher likely knew this would be the outcome from the very beginning. That I couldn't save her, and that I'd be with her in her final moments. Which was why she told me that the more I tried to fight fate, the more I would be the one who ended up getting hurt.

I could only imagine that my teacher had gone through a similar experience herself. That she didn't want me to suffer the same pain she did.

"The weight of the day many people will never get the chance to see—you carry that weight on your shoulders. This is why you must live on. For those who've died, and those who are still here. This is your duty as someone who knows the dead."

"Yes..."

"We should tell the family."

"I'll go."

I looked my teacher straight in the eyes. I'm sure my face was all scrunched up, as I tried to control my emotions. Though I wouldn't be surprised if some snot managed to escape. Nevertheless, I managed to hold back my tears.

"It's something I should do."

I'd yet to find a real purpose in my life. By seeing someone important to me leave this world, though, I felt like I'd finally realized it.

The sunlight was warm as it shone down on us, and the air was filled with a child's laughter. With a blue sky and a soft breeze, it was one of the best days in what was normally a cold month—and as good a day as there could be for a nice old lady to pass away.

Her name was Flaire. She loved gardening and was like a grandmother to me. She was always nice to everyone and took me in generously whenever I needed her.

I'll live a full life, for both of us. I'll start by deciding tonight's dinner: a nice warm pot of beef stew. Tomorrow, I think I'll make some rosemary cookies. We can enjoy them together because your memory will always live on inside me.

For as long as I live, we'll be together.

Chapter 5:
Blessings
and the
Open Portal

It wasn't long before Lapis was well into the winter. It was that time of year when your breath turns white and you struggle to get out of your warm bed in the morning.

In Lapis, we had a special event that took place this time of year. This was opening a portal that led to other worlds. By connecting our world with others, we could welcome otherworldly guests.

Long ago in Japan, there used to be a system known as *sakoku*—a policy to isolate the country from the rest of the world. During that time, the only part of the country to have any interaction with the outside world was a single island in its southern archipelago. What Lapis did was similar; we opened up our world to another in only this spot.

Setting aside the festival itself, this was the time of year when Lapis shone most. Magic flowed throughout the town, and people from other worlds mingled with the citizens of our own. The event was only possible because this town was under the jurisdiction of one of the Seven Sages, and the event was known as the "Celebration of Worlds."

With my teacher obviously being the Sage who oversaw the festival, it was also one of the busiest times of year for her.

"Um..."

I made a sound of confusion, to which my teacher responded with "Pipe down, Meg. What are you moaning and groaning about on your computer? If you have time to grumble, get to answering some e-mails."

It was all hands on deck at the Faust manor, where every witch and familiar had a task assigned to them. And believe me, there were no shortages of tasks. The familiars gathered the materials and resources we needed for the festival, and my teacher handled all the paperwork. I, on the other hand, was on computer duty, answering the never-ending chain of e-mails while also helping my teacher with magic formula preparation.

There were many rules set in place for interacting with the other worlds, and the e-mails were mostly questions about these among a laundry list of others.

The issue was, I was in no place to be handling these tasks.

"Teacher, you need to see this."

I shifted my computer screen toward her, and she curiously approached to watch. On the screen was an article about a young woman. She had lush blue hair, red eyes, and an intelligent-looking face. It was this, and the fleeting sense of melancholy that lingered in her expression, that had the world so captivated.

"Is that the Sage Sophie?"

"Yes."

Also known by her witch name, the Witch of Blessings, Sophie was one of the Seven Sages. She was a genius if there ever was one, having taken one of the seats at the table of the Seven Sages at the young age of seventeen.

Evidently, she was in South America for a festival the month before, where a grand parade took place.

"What's the issue with her?"

"Isn't it obvious? She's the same age as me! And we're both witches! And yet she's all over the net, where they're calling her things like *princess*! Mind tellin' me why *I'm* not one of the Seven Sages yet?"

"Because you lack knowledge and ability. You're also less

virtuous than Sophie—and, let's face it, a bit more homely than she is."

"Enough! You've made your point!"

Reality is a cruel mistress.

Sophie was essentially the perfect witch I wanted to be, and there she was, on my computer screen.

I was an apprentice witch stuck in the countryside, and she was one of the Seven Sages, who acted on the world stage.

Realistically, we both probably started learning magic around the same time, and yet we both ended up in entirely different places in our lives.

My teacher sighed wearily as she watched me gnash my teeth at the picture.

"I was wondering what was keeping you from getting your work done. So you're jealous of Sophie, are you? Listen, Meg. No two people are the same. Everyone has something they excel at, as well as things that are not their specialty. Comparing yourself to others does nothing for you. What matters is accomplishing what you can and should. Doing so will take you where you need to go, eventually."

"Eventually, eh...?"

"Speaking of which, have you managed to accumulate more tears of joy?"

"I have eleven..."

The extra tears were from random deeds of kindness, like helping a small child find his mother or helping an elderly person find something they lost.

Unlike *Sophie*, I had to run around the countryside like some salesman to earn my quota in tears.

"Jealousy is the last thing you have time for right now. Your highest priority should be survival. Or else you have no future either way."

"I know..."

I had a tab open with a video of Sophie using her magic. It looked like a video made with CG, with the way beams of light shot up, bird illusions flew about, and the stars in the night sky twinkled. Flames turned from red to green, and the lights in the room turned every which color—all the effects controlled by a single witch.

If I could do that, I bet I could get all the tears I need.

All the thoughts that surged through my mind were anything *but* constructive.

"If you understand, then go get my things ready. We only have a week left."

"Righto."

Hearing my unenthusiastic response, my teacher simply shrugged and left me to my desk work. A significant amount of time passed before I realized I'd been scrolling through video after video. They'd taken all my attention, making me forget about the tasks at hand.

She wanted me to get her things, right?

I closed my laptop and stood up, and suddenly an ominous snapping sound rang out.

All familiar eyes were on me.

"Huh? Was that me?"

I searched my body, but there was nothing wrong. That's when I heard the horrible shrill of a woman screaming for her life. The awful shriek sent the familiars running off in every direction in fear.

With caution, I steeled my nerves and approached the area where the shriek had come from. It was a desk. I gulped as I walked toward it. Familiars had gathered, watching from behind the door to the next room, each waiting for whatever was about to unfold.

The source of the voice was lying on the ground…

"Oh, it's just you."

"What's that supposed to mean, you insensitive piece of...?"

My teacher was lying on the ground, surrounded by boxes and cases. It looked like she had tried to carry her things on her own.

"You're way too old to be doing that. Can you walk?"

"I don't think I can. I may have thrown my back out... Ow..."

I lent her a shoulder to help her get up, and she painfully put a hand to her lower back. It didn't look like she'd be able to walk. For now, I took her to bed, careful not to stimulate the wounded area.

In that moment, it had yet to occur to me that the Celebration of Worlds had just lost its host.

○

"Ow, ow, ow, ouch! Be careful with my back!"

"Toughen up, buttercup."

The familiars watched from the corner while I placed an herbal patch on the spot where it hurt on my teacher's back as she lay in bed. Though it was a special, magically enhanced patch, it would take some time for her back to completely heal.

"The town doctor should be here soon, so just try to get some rest."

Normally, I would poke fun at my teacher in such a vulnerable state, but this time it was me at fault for slacking off on the job and making her carry the boxes in the first place.

It was times like these when I had to wonder why she didn't use magic to move the boxes, though. She was one of the Seven Sages, after all. Moving things and cleaning up rooms was rudimentary magic.

I knew she never would, though. While it was true that using magic took a toll on the body in a different way, she was the type who wanted to use her hands to do manual labor such as chores and shopping.

This philosophy went beyond magic. In modern times, electronic goods supplemented people in the same way magic did. The right combination of tools was all one needed to make their life much easier. Easy wasn't always the answer; skimping out on chores was a quick way to fall out of shape, age faster, and dull the mind. This was why my teacher taught me that it was important to do such chores with my own two hands.

It was an outdated way of thinking based on the witches of old. I didn't hate the idea, though. And because I understood this aspect of my teacher and appreciated it, I should've done the job before she needed to.

"This puts us in a bit of a bind. What are we going to do about the portal? It needs to open next week."

"Uh-oh…"

She was right. The biggest event of the year, the Celebration of Worlds, was just around the corner, and it wouldn't be much of a Celebration of Worlds without an open portal. That wasn't all; magic was accumulating around Lapis for the event, and it needed to be used somehow. Connecting our world to others was important for this reason as well.

That said, opening the portal wasn't something I could ever do. Though I helped my teacher with the event every year, the feat wasn't something a mere apprentice could ever dream of pulling off.

"We're gonna have to cancel it, I guess?"

"Then what will we do with the unused magic?"

"Maybe we could use it for a different event?"

"Many people wait all year for this event; you know that, Meg."

"Yeah, hmm."

I crossed my arms and groaned in thought, when my teacher looked up and said, "Well…we may need to call in a substitute."

"And who's that?"

"You'll find out soon enough. For now, make sure you finish

up all your assigned tasks by the day of the event. We wouldn't want it being canceled for an unrelated reason."

"Okay..."

Though I didn't like being brushed off like this, I went back to my post and picked up where I'd left off.

Is it really going to be okay? I'll have to worry about it later. For now, I need to get this work done.

"Yeah, sometimes people die, and things just don't work out."

"I'm not dead yet."

The next morning, I woke up to an unexpected frigidness—or more like the frigidness woke me. I'd nodded off while finishing some paperwork, but the office was so cold that I could almost see my breath. Then I noticed the weight. My body felt heavy; it was a horde of familiars and Carbuncle huddled up next to me to keep me warm. If I didn't end up getting a cold from sleeping in the study, it would be thanks to these little guys.

I looked over to the window, where White-Owl was sitting. Our eyes locked.

"Mornin'."

"Hoot."

"Sure is chilly today."

I shook off my familiar-fur coat and picked up a bottle of magical herbs. Shivering, I brought the bottle into the next room, where I would use the herbs as fuel for a fire. The halls of the manor were as icy as its study in the early morning. The floor creaked with each step I took on its cold surface, and I could feel my body temperature lowering from my feet.

I powered through the trek into the living room, passed the girl sitting in the chair, and headed straight for the fireplace. There, I used magic to ignite a combination of firewood and crumpled-up newspapers.

"Whew, it's freezing in here."

Something occurred to me as I said this.

Wait, huh?

"Was there a girl just now…?"

"Hi."

"Waaagh!"

I lost my footing from the shock, falling to the ground as the girl stood up from her chair.

"What are you doing?"

"No! What are *you* doing *here*?!"

In the next moment, I realized the girl looked familiar.

"Wait…"

Lush blue hair and pearl-white skin. A perfect, out-of-a-princess-movie face. Somewhat jarring red eyes.

It was the Witch of Blessings, Sophie—the witch I'd seen on television so many times and always wished I could be.

"T-Teeeacheeerrr!"

I opened the door into my teacher's room and was greeted with "You're loud this morning" by my teacher, who had turned to look over from her bed.

"Meg, please come and rub my back."

"Y-you got it."

Was it sad? I couldn't really say no to my teacher, even at times like this.

"Wait! Before that!"

I smacked the bed.

"Th-th-there's a ghost! In our living room! It looks like Sophie!"

"She's already here? That was sooner than I expected."

"Come again?"

As I questioned my teacher, I felt a presence behind me. Cautiously, I turned around…and there she was. The ghost of Sophie.

"Th-there it is again!"

Too afraid to think straight, I grabbed on to my teacher right on her waist where it hurt the most, and she let out what sounded like it could be her dying wail. "Graaaagh!"

"I'm here, Faust."

She wasn't a ghost. The girl from the video with seventy-something million plays I'd watched the day prior was standing here, in our old country manor.

○

"She'll be standing in for you?"

I set a cup of tea down on my teacher's desk for Sophie, and my teacher quietly replied, "Yes," and nodded before taking a sip of the tea. "It's a busy time of year. There are lots of requests being made regarding the festival. It's a trade. In exchange for letting her stay with us for a while, she will open the portal in my stead. My back should be better by the end of the festival. It worked out for her since London is close to Lapis."

So that was why she'd contacted Sophie, one of the Seven Sages. Needless to say, this wasn't something that could usually be done on a whim.

"Sometimes I forget you're one of the Seven Sages."

"What's that supposed to mean…? Listen, Meg. It doesn't look like I'll be up and about anytime soon, so I'll need you to assist Sophie."

"You want me to do what?"

I couldn't believe my ears.

"Yes. You know everything about the town and the festival. You'll be her assistant this year, as you usually are for me."

"Uhhh…"

The girl genius witch needed my help? It was a good opportunity, but one that came with immense pressure. Were Sophie to be in charge of opening Lapis's portal, it would draw attention from around the world. The festival would be busier than normal, which would only increase the likelihood of a mishap. If I somehow screwed something up, it would rub dirt in both my teacher's and Sophie's faces.

I was pretty terrified on the inside, which my teacher saw right through, prompting a grin on her face.

"Sophie is a genius. Learn everything you can from her."

"O-okay."

My teacher had a way of slamming me with the most troublesome tasks imaginable. I breathed a small sigh and turned to find Sophie looking at me. She had teardrop-shaped eyes, flawless pale skin, and silky blue hair. It was like looking at fresh snow. Sophie cut off my moment of being captivated by her looks by muttering, "I'd like to see it. The spot where I'm going to open the portal."

"Oh, sure. You want to see the spot where you're gonna work, eh? I'll take you there. My name is Meg Raspberry, by the way."

"Nice to meet you, Spberry."

"It's Raspberry..."

We were walking down the road along the river that took us to Lapis. There were clouds in the sky—it looked like it might snow—and a significant part of the river was frozen over. As I shivered in the frigid cold, it occurred to me that I was walking next to a celebrity.

The Seven Sages were famous, but Sophie was on a level of her own in terms of fame. Though the other six Sages were closer to scholars than celebs, Sophie was constantly on television and had many fans; she stood out the most.

The reason for her fame was her history and the type of work she did. A young prodigy, she excelled academically in the same way she did with magic, entering one of the world's most prestigious universities to study physics at a young age. After graduating, she went on to become a performer who traveled the world instead of going down the research route. She used powerful light magic to create firework-like shows of magical explosions and flashes, often during magic parades, wherever she went.

Her unique head of blue hair and rare eyes were an oddity that was generally considered very beautiful, and it didn't take long for her to gain popularity, to the point where not a day went by when I didn't see her on television or web news.

She was the most famous person on the planet at the moment—a young witch prodigy named Sophie Hayter. I'd only ever seen her on a screen up until now, but there she was, walking right next to me.

"Wow, sure is a cold one today, isn't it? It doesn't look like it's bothering you much, though. Aren't you cold, Sophie?"

"Not particularly."

As I asked her this, I thought about how her snow-like appearance matched perfectly with the weather, but I kept this thought to myself.

She and I were the same age, but there was something about how she held herself that surpassed her years—like a sort of presence. She had this aura to her, just like my teacher and Inori had to them, but there was something different about the vibe she gave off. I usually didn't have a difficult time getting along with anyone, even if it was our first meeting, but something about her felt unapproachable. Like there was a wall between us. Maybe it was an aura unique to geniuses?

"What?"

Uh-oh. I'd been staring too much, and now she was looking directly back at me. I froze up and let out an awkward "Ha-ha-ha" as a nervous habit.

"Sorry, I was just thinking about how pretty you are. I love your blue hair."

"I see."

And then there was silence—awkward silence.

"It must be tough for you this time of year, with all the parades going on. You know, I actually saw a video of your last one. Wow, it sure was awesome. It's crazy to think we're both the same age. I guess geniuses are just built different, eh? Ha-ha-ha-ha."

"Yeah."

Nothing I said got a reaction out of her.

"Hey, Spberry."

"It's Raspberry."

"Do you have your witch name yet?"

"My witch name? I'm still a rookie."

"The Rookie Witch, Spberry."

"That's not my witch name or my real name," I jokingly retorted.

But without the slightest hint of a smile, Sophie tonelessly responded, "Oh." If that was how she was going to react, it would've been better if she didn't ask at all. This sentiment must've been written on my face, because as soon as she turned and saw my expression, she continued. "Seeing as you're the witch Faust's apprentice, I simply thought it wouldn't be out of the realm of possibility for you to have one."

"Do you think they're all that necessary?"

"There are many witches who don't have their names yet, but having one is proof that people value your ability."

This wasn't untrue. Having a witch name was a high honor, but they were usually only given to people on par with the caliber of the Seven Sages, who had incredible accomplishments under their belts—not something I was even close to having yet.

As I pondered over it, a motorbike traveling the opposite direction came up on us. We got out of the way, but instead of passing us, the bike slowed to a stop.

"Hello, Miss Meg. Funny running into you here like this."

It was the son of the town's baker, Onnet.

"Oh, it's you. You helping your parents? Well, aren't you a good son?"

"Heh, yeah."

Onnet bashfully rubbed his nose but then noticed Sophie next to me.

"Who's your friend?

"It's our guest. Well, my teacher's."

"Lady Faust has a guest?"

Onnet's expression lit up. With a quivering arm, he pointed straight at Sophie.

That's rude.

"She has blue hair and red eyes… She doesn't happen to be… Sophie Hayter…?"

"You bet she is. My teacher hurt her back, so we need her help opening the portal this year."

"Whoa, you're the real thing!"

Onnet looked at her and then back at me; his eyes twinkled with envy and respect. Sophie, on the other hand, seemed somewhat uncomfortable with the exchange. She probably wasn't a fan of having people recognize her.

"Could I, uh, shake your hand?"

Sophie hesitated at first but slowly extended her hand for a shake. He grabbed her hand, and his face lit up like a Christmas tree.

"Geez, I just shook Sophie's hand! The Sophie! I'm never gonna wash this hand again."

"You're a baker, so I hope you wash it for your customers' sake. Aren't you supposed to be on the job?"

"Oh crap! I have a delivery to make! Well, I'll see you later, Miss Sophie! I'm gonna make you some delicious bread, and then—"

"All right, all right! Just hurry up and get back to work already!"

"On it!"

We watched as Onnet drove his motorbike away, becoming smaller and smaller as he went on.

"He's like a bull in a china shop, he is. Sorry, us country folk get pretty excited when we meet famous people."

"It's fine."

As she said this, Sophie was staring at the hand she'd used to shake Onnet's. There was a somewhat sad look in her eyes.

"You okay? Miss Sophie? I don't think you have to worry about his hand. He probably washes it after using the loo 'cause he's a baker and everything."

"I'm not concerned about that. It's fine… Let's go."

"Oh, okay."

I watched as Sophie quickly continued down the path.

It wouldn't be later until I learned the truth behind her sad expression.

As soon as we reached the town, Sophie suddenly stopped walking.

"Something wrong?"

"I just need a moment."

She then began running her hand through her hair like a comb. I watched as in an instant, her hair turned from blue to brown. The same went for her red eyes, which lost their hue and changed to a much duller color.

I was astonished; it was a technique I'd never seen before.

"Because of that boy from before."

"You mean Onnet? I guess if people realized you were in town, it could draw a crowd. We're all country bumpkins around here… But isn't it a bit of a shame? To have to dye your pretty blue hair."

"The effect is only temporary. It doesn't even last long."

After she said this, she pinched a lock of her hair.

"There's no escaping this hair and eye color of mine."

"What's that supposed to mean?"

She didn't answer this question. Instead, she opted to leave me standing there confused over the remark, which sounded like something an emo teenager would say.

When we made our way to the market, we were met by an endless stream of people who called out to me.

"Hey, it's Lady Faust's apprentice. You out on an errand?"

"Yup."

"If it isn't the disciple! Are you here with your friend?"

"Heh-heh. Sure am!"

"It's the witch! Hey, let's play!"

"Sorry, but I have something I need to do. Next time, okay?"

"It's the apprentice witch girl! Nanny-nanny boo-boo, you're *uuuuggglllllyyy*!"

"Listen here, you little brats! I'll gather all the human and cow poo in this town, boil it in a big pot for three days, and throw you in it!! What do ya think of that, huh?!"

I continued to exchange salutations with everyone we met as we made our way to the town square, and just as Sophie intended, not a single person paid any attention to her.

"Sorry about all the chatter."

"Is it like this for you whenever you come to town?"

"Yeah, I guess. It's a small town, so you can't take a few steps without running into someone you know."

"Is that so…?"

Sophie said this, then turned her attention to the marketplace.

"Uh… Something catch your interest? You seem lost in thought."

"It's nothing. I was just thinking about the name they were using."

"Did you want to know one of their names?"

"No. Your name. Not a single person called you Spberry."

"Huh? Well, now that you mention it..."

I never really thought about it, but people around here never called me Meg Raspberry. It was always *Lady Faust's apprentice*.

"I guess my teacher *is* one of the Seven Sages, after all. But it has its upsides, too. Thanks to that, I know pretty much everyone around here."

"Is that right?"

Sophie gave me a look that could only be described as entirely disinterested.

"I understand now why you've yet to acquire a witch name."

"Huh?"

"It's because no one recognizes you as a witch."

Sophie muttered this before continuing to walk toward the town square. I, however, stood in that spot, alone.

"What's her deal...?"

She's so abrasive. It's like she's judging me. I wonder what she doesn't like about me. I can't tell what she's thinking or read her face at all.

As I pondered this, we eventually made it to the town square.

"This is the largest open space in the entire town and where we'll be opening the portal."

The town square was smack-dab in the center of Lapis and was a popular spot for events and lounging about. There were often flea markets and live shows held during the weekends, and it was where many elderly citizens gathered to socialize, young people danced, and...well, a lot of people used this space. Our job was to connect this world with the other worlds by constructing a giant portal here.

Sophie then walked forward and began using her hand to draw an arch in the air. As her hand moved through the air, light followed it, which made me audibly gasp.

"Whoa! What are you doing?"

"I'm creating a hypothetical construction of the portal."

"What? Already?"

We hadn't even been there for a minute yet. I still needed to tell her about various intricacies needed to make the portal, such as the type of magic in the dirt. I could only imagine what was going on in that head of hers; it astonished me.

Sophie and I were cut from fundamentally different cloth. This was what it meant to be a genius. To be born with natural talent.

After she finished drawing her magic circle in the air, she activated it. An illusion of the portal then appeared. It was like a real-life hologram, showing a portal large enough for three or four people to pass comfortably through at a time.

"Is this about the right size?"

"It is… Uh, is this the same magic you use during parades?"

"Yes, it is illusionary magic."

During the parades Sophie helped throw, she manifested and controlled multiple phenomenal magic spells at the same time, or so I'd read on a magic-related message board. This meant she needed to construct, activate, and control multiple magical formulas at the same time. It was like holding an orchestra where you were both the conductor and playing every instrument all at once—not something a normal person could do.

It was the reason her parades always moved people to tears, and I thought to myself…

She truly is one of a kind. Normally, I'd feel depressed seeing someone my age doing so much better than me, but I can't afford to let this opportunity pass by. I need to learn from her, if I can. I'd have to be an idiot to just sit here and feel bad for myself.

"Can I ask you a question?"

"What?"

"How did you learn to do all this?"

"It's a simple principle. First, you must understand physics and chemistry. Once you have a thorough understanding of these both, use them for magic. It isn't difficult to formulate spells as long as you have a basic understanding of the elements at hand."

"Yeah, that sounds impossible."

It was like we were in two different dimensions. What was I supposed to learn from a genius?

Our conversation was cut short by a loud, sudden sound.

Gurrrrgggle, rumble, rummmble, guuurrrgle.

Listen to that, oof. Someone must be having a really bad day with their digestive system, I thought, then noticed that Sophie had her hand on her stomach.

"I'm hungry."

"That was *your* stomach?"

It then occurred to me that we hadn't eaten anything all morning. I was also pretty hungry.

"I know, I'll take you to one of my favorite places."

"Oh?"

We walked a short distance to a nearby bakery that was just next to the town square. This bakery had a small café inside it, allowing customers to eat the bread they purchased in the store. I proceeded to sit and watch Sophie stuff her small mouth with a sandwich. She looked like a hamster with cheeks full of food. Watching Sophie like this made her look younger than she already was. Younger than me, at least, and definitely younger than the witch the world was enthralled with.

"Ish tayshdtea."

"I have no idea what you just said."

"This is very tasty."

"Right? This bakery is run by Onnet's parents. The kid on the bike we met earlier."

Sophie scanned the bakery while she enjoyed a cup of black

tea. It was a weekday morning, so we had the café to ourselves. We were the only customers in the store. The background music was a soft jazz track, and there was a large window from which we could watch the town's main street.

We watched a busy-looking businessman rushing down the sidewalk, a mum pushing a baby in a stroller, and an old woman walking with a cane. They were all citizens of this town, and this was their everyday life.

"This is a nice town. It's so peaceful here, and everyone is nice."

"That's what makes small towns great."

What felt like a pretty mundane response left Sophie with a somewhat sad, empty look. She gave off the same sense of loneliness that cold winter days brought with them.

"Hey, Spberry."

"Raspberry."

"Why did you decide to learn magic?"

"Huh?"

I was caught off guard by the sudden question.

"You're learning magic under Faust. Why?"

"Why? Uh, I don't know. It just kind of happened."

"What do you mean?"

"I'm an orphan. My parents died before I was old enough to remember them. Child protection services was going to put me in an orphanage, but my teacher came along and took me in before that happened. She's been my mum ever since, and learning magic was just a part of living with her. I've been doing it since before I could walk."

"You're an orphan…"

"I read online that you studied magic from a very young age, too."

"Yes, out of necessity…"

"You needed to study magic?"

What could that mean? There was a lot unknown about

Sophie's birth. She was a genius unlike anyone the world had ever known, and she'd appeared out of nowhere. There wasn't anything online about her past from before she was a mage. This mysterious part of her may have been another reason for her popularity.

"Is there something you'd like to use magic for, Spberry?"

"Money, money, money," I said without hesitation, but continued. "Oh, but…"

"But?"

"Before that, I need to stay alive."

"Stay alive?"

"Yeah. I need to live a long life if I want to do anything. I don't want to forget about all the people who've been important in my life."

At this rate, I only had about ten months left to live. I knew, though, that I would do anything to keep myself from dying. There were things I wanted to accomplish and people I still wanted to get to know better. I realized there were a lot of reasons I needed to continue living.

"That's quaint, Spberry."

"Raspberry."

"That is a bit too much for using magic, though."

"What do you mean?"

Sophie turned to me and looked me right in the eyes.

"You don't need magic to do any of that."

"Huh?"

"Making money and living a long life are both things that can be done entirely without the use of magic. You are studying magic without a clear reason to do so. This is the reason no one recognizes you as a witch, despite learning under Faust."

"So what's your goal in learning magic?"

Sophie's eyes seemed to darken before she answered.

"My goal…is to eliminate magic from this world."

Her expression was gloomier than anything I'd seen from her yet.

"Magic has taken everything away from me, so I want to remove its existence. That is why I've studied it."

I couldn't believe what I was hearing. The Witch of Blessings, the person who had moved so many people in the entire world to tears with her magic, wanted to get rid of it all together? I wanted it to be a joke, but I could tell by her tone that she was sincere.

"You're in the same situation as me, so I will let you in on a secret about magic, Spberry. You need to throw away everything if you hope to truly acquire the ability to cast magic."

"Everything...?"

"Everything. Your family, home, friends, dreams. You throw it all away just to achieve your goal—that is how you acquire magic quickly."

"Slow down, Sophie. You're laying it on thick."

"Yooouuu haaavvvee tooo giiivvve uuup eeeveryyythiii..."

"What are you doing now?"

"I'm slowing down for you."

"That's not what I meant."

In that moment, I felt a presence behind us. Startled, I turned around to find Onnet acting a bit fidgety.

"Oh! Onnet. Hey, we came for some bread."

I noticed that there he was again, pointing that old finger of his with an excited tremble, at Sophie.

I'd better tell him not to point at people next time. I'd like to see the look on his parents' faces.

I looked over at the cash register, and there was his mum. She didn't seem to notice her son. Oh well.

"Is that brown-haired girl...Sophie Hayter...?"

"Yeah. I thought we established that already?"

"Yeah, but her hair is all different... I can't believe you're here eating bread at my family's bakery… You look pretty as a brunette, too…"

"Stop, you're gonna creep her out."

I breathed a sigh of exasperation at his behavior. Thanks to him, the conversation we were having had come to an abrupt end. Sophie continued to drink tea, like the exchange never even happened.

I couldn't stop thinking about it, though…the brief moment of darkness she showed me.

It felt almost like I'd caught a glimpse of Sophie's true self.

○

"Eliminate magic, eh…?"

Lying on my bed, I stared at the ceiling as I mumbled to myself. Carbuncle was hunkered down next to me, looking at my face. I started petting him, and he closed his eyes in delight.

Sophie said that magic took everything away from her. Despite traveling the world and giving people hope everywhere she went, she said she'd lost something. I didn't know what she truly meant by that, but I felt like I could maybe understand why. Had magic never existed, my life would look very different than it did now. I certainly wouldn't be cursed, for example, and maybe I would be a regular student at a normal school. Life would be more peaceful and less of a struggle for me—it would be normal.

At the same time, I thought that without magic, there was a lot I never would've attained. Knowing all the people in town, or Inori or Sophie, for that matter. I wouldn't have Carbuncle rubbing his head against me or White-Owl watching patiently from the windowsill, and I may have never been adopted by my teacher.

One thing was certain in that case. Meg Raspberry, the witch, would never exist.

There were two sides to everything in life. This was something my teacher had taught me before.

It was true—the existence of magic had harmed me in many ways. But it had also given me so much.

"Argh, I have no idea what to think. Let's go get some tea."

"*Squeak.*"

Carbuncle hopped onto my shoulder, and we went to the living room to put some water in the pot. Then my teacher showed up going, "Owww, ouch, ouch…"

"Hey, Teacher. You're standing already?"

"Yes, barely… It's thanks to your medicine patch."

"I'm glad I could help. Fancy some tea?"

"I would, thank you."

I poured two cups of black tea, and we let out puffs of white-hot breath as we drank them together. There was nothing better than warm tea on a cold winter day, something my teacher always said.

"Where is Sophie?"

"She's asleep in the guest room. She passed out as soon as we got home."

"She must be awfully knackered."

"Was Sophie always like that, Teacher?"

"What do you mean?"

"She looks so lonely, like she's living in her own world or something. I'm guessing it has to do with how she hates magic and all that, though."

When I said this, my teacher said, "Perhaps…" and stared off into the distance, then continued. "She was like that when we first met, too. Always staying away from people and keeping to herself."

"Sophie said she wants to eliminate magic and that I *have* too much to learn it properly."

"Is that right...? I suppose you may seem that way from her perspective."

"What do you mean?"

"Do you know how old Sophie was when she left her family, Meg?"

"I thought it was when she became a Sage, at seventeen."

"It was when she was five."

"Five?!"

"She was too smart for her own good. Smarter than anyone. And nobody wanted to accept her for who she was."

Sophie was born in northern Europe with powerful magic inside her, which was what turned her hair blue and her eyes red. It was said, though, that because of her hair, Sophie's parents thought she was the devil's child. Nevertheless, her birth parents tried to take care of her, or so it was said.

It wouldn't take long for them to discover, however, that it wasn't just her hair and eyes that differed from regular children.

"Mum... Dad..."

Sophie spoke her first words when she was one year old. When most one-year-old babies were barely talking at all, she could have a full conversation. By the time she was two, she could read and do math as well.

That wasn't all, though.

"Who's that boy standing there?"

Sophie started saying things like this by the time she was three. She would point to a spot where there was nobody and claim to see someone. Her parents thought she was playing a joke on them at first.

"Sophie. What did you do with the plates I left here?"

"The boy from before took them to the sink."

"Not that again..."

In the next instant, the sound of a plate shattering on the floor rang out through the house. The parents went to see what it was, and there was a broken plate in the sink. The same plate Sophie and her mum were talking about before.

Strange occurrences like this started to happen more frequently, and Sophie's parents began to find her unsettling. It wasn't just her parents; everyone in Sophie's life began to distance themselves from her.

Sophie was alone. It was around this time when she began to take an interest in magic and harnessed it with what knowledge she'd gathered on her own. It was likely that she just wanted to impress her parents, but in the north, where magic wasn't as accepted as it was in the rest of the world, she was labeled a demon and hated for it.

She was all alone, seeing things no one else could see and using power no one understood.

Eventually, the Council of Magic found their way to Sophie, took her in, and had her undergo a special curriculum to learn about magic. Something her parents were overjoyed about.

My teacher just so happened to be working at the facility as a temporary teacher when this happened.

"When I first saw Sophie, it struck me how sad she looked. She had to accept the fact that she was abandoned at such a young age because of magic. Magic changed her life. It was what she was best at but also what made the people she loved most discard her."

"I don't know what to say..."

"From the perspective of someone who feels truly alone, you may look very privileged. Despite coming from a similar place, you are surrounded by people. What Sophie needed was people who understood magic and accepted her when she was younger."

"So that's why she hates magic."

I'd misunderstood everything about her. I'd assumed she was from a wealthy family that helped her with her magic studies from a very young age, but it was the opposite. Though she did receive an advanced curriculum for her magic from a very young age, she must have felt conflicted by it because magic was what drove those she loved away from her.

"My goal is to eliminate magic from this world."

That was what Sophie told me. My best guess was that she believed eliminating magic would allow her to live with her family once more. This was surely the reason she'd decided to lean into magic and to become one of the world's greatest witches. Sophie had nothing left but her magic, after all. Her only option was to build on what she had.

In that same vein, it must've been difficult for her to accept that I could study magic without any real purpose and have a place to call home.

She told me that having nothing was the key to learning magic fast. Though there may have been some logic to that, was it really the case?

"I still have one question. Why does Sophie use her magic for performances and shows despite hating it so much? It feels like her use of magic draws more attention to it than anything else."

Hearing this, my teacher answered with a sad expression, "She likely wants someone to notice her," before continuing. "She may try to isolate herself, but I know somewhere on the inside, she still desires other people in her life. That is why she chose to use her magic in a way that made the most people happy. Maybe she wants her parents to accept her for who she is, too. She is trying to use magic to take back what it took away from her."

"With magic..."

Sophie was a genius with drive, but she also had a hard time vocalizing her ideas. She must've put everything into learning magic, like her life depended on it—like she was desperate.

No... She's still desperate.

"Listen to me, Meg. You are nothing compared to Sophie. An idiot who grew up in the best environment imaginable for learning magic. You're loud and crude, with your skills in the kitchen being your only saving grace."

"I think you're taking this a little bit too far..."

"But you have something she doesn't."

"And that is...?"

"You both grew up in similar situations, but you never allowed yourself to harbor hatred for it. You have light in your heart. A warm light—warmth that can melt Sophie's frozen heart."

My teacher said this and smiled a smile that made me sigh. It was another unmanageable task.

It's not easy opening someone up, you know.

That said, I wasn't the type to let Sophie leave Lapis feeling like this. She was such an incredible witch, which wasn't just my opinion, either; the entire world adored her, and I wasn't going to let her feel alone.

○

The next day, Sophie and I began the preparations together. There were seven layers to the magic formula needed for Sophie to open the portal, each requiring materials that needed to be gathered from throughout the town.

Though this was something we did every year, it was impossible to use the same formula. This was because the magic that flowed through the town and its surrounding environment was ever-changing. Building even just one new building, for example, completely changed the formula. This was how meticulous a process it was to open the portal to other worlds.

"Here you go, Meg! I brought you some snacks!"

"Oh! Thanks, Fine!"

My best friend came bearing tea and bread she'd purchased at the local supermarket.

"I heard about Lady Faust. That she hurt her back. Are you going to be okay on your own?"

"Heh-heh, get this. We have a special super-powerful friend here to help."

"A friend?"

"Spberry. Where did you put the bronze?"

With a nicely timed question, Sophie drew Fine's attention, making her eyes go wide with surprise.

"A-are you Sophie? Like, one of the Seven Sages?"

"Indeed I am."

Fine let out a whimper of "Oh…," and I put my hand on her shoulder.

"I can feel butterflies in my stomach."

"Here, I'll smoosh them for you."

"Please stop that."

A few more days of this passed. With the first and second formulas completed, it was crunch time for the portal.

After spending a few days with Sophie, I realized two things about her. First, that her knowledge when it came to both magic and academics was the real deal. And second, that there was someone who knew even more than she did, and that was the Eternal Witch, Faust.

Sophie's position as a Sage was not misguided; she had the technical skills and mind for it. But even so, there were many areas where it felt like my teacher was a much better mage. It was a good reminder of how incredible the person I learned under truly was.

Though we were both filled with energy at the beginning of the portal's construction, by the time we made it to the seventh formula, the process was starting to take its toll on us. Even Sophie, who always had the same expression on her face, couldn't hide her fatigue.

"We will be constructing the seventh formula today."

"Uh-huh."

Sophie used her pointer finger to draw out a magic circle in the air in front of her, simulating the effect of its magical reaction. Thinking back on it, I saw Inori do something similar. They both managed to whip up very complex formulas in a matter of seconds.

If Sophie was using the same methodology as Inori, there must've been a rhyme and reason to it.

"How do you draw out formulas with your hand like that?"

"It takes two steps. First, you bring your magic to your fingertip to give it the same effect as chanting. Then you release that magic to create a flow that makes up the formula. Executing these two steps in as little time as possible also serves to shorten the casting process."

"Yeah, that sounds pretty impossible."

I tried it a few times, but nothing happened. I wasn't even sure what it was supposed to feel like accumulating my magic into my fingertip.

"This is tough."

"Practice makes perfect."

"Right."

I decided to practice more when I got home. With that in mind, I noticed the formula Sophie was in the process of constructing, and something felt off about it.

"Did you change the formula?"

This question seemed to confuse Sophie, who cocked her head to the side and asked:

"What makes you think that?"

"I just thought it looked a bit different from how we usually do it. I mean, this part is very different, and look over here. Here, it's supposed to stabilize this world's connection with the others, right? I don't think you're supposed to mix these two types of formulas with each other; they clash."

Hearing my point made Sophie go quiet for a few moments. Perhaps due to always helping my teacher with these formulas every year, a part of me was confident in my understanding of the formulas that made connecting multiple worlds possible. Which was why even though I didn't completely understand the physics behind it, I could tell something was off.

"What made you want to change the formula?"

"I wanted to make the portal bigger."

"Bigger? What was wrong with its normal size?"

"I researched the data from previous years, and it was clear to me that the number of visitors coming through the portal every year is rising. While using the same formula to make the portal this year would be stable, it wouldn't be large enough to allow everyone through."

"I see. You have a point there."

During the Celebration of Worlds, a wide variety of citizens from many other worlds came here. She must've thought it would be more convenient to make a larger portal. It might have been her own way of trying to make this festival even better.

The problem was that the larger the portal, the less firm the magic would be as it took hold, making it difficult to control the amount of power. This would require adding yet another formula to ensure the portal's stability, which was apt to create another scenario where two formulas clashed. It would be like using a water formula to control a fire spell; it may result in certain parts of the formula disappearing entirely.

"It will work this way. Don't worry."

"Are you sure?"

"I've used much larger formulas than this before. I'm capable of creating the portal at the size we need it."

I doubted her. At the very least, my teacher had never created a portal this large before. She always placed more emphasis on safety, after all.

"You may be right about the portal being too small in terms of the scale of the event, but one thing is for sure: It's stable. We can't afford for the portal we create to be unstable, so if we're going to change it, I think it would be best to ask my teacher first."

Sophie shook her head upon hearing this.

"It will be all right. I'd rather not depend on Faust. This formula will work. I'm sure of it. I guarantee it. I'll bet my life on it."

"You should value your life more."

It almost looked like Sophie was hesitating about something. I didn't know what kind of person she was, or anything much about her at all, but I knew she wasn't an idiot. Sure, she believed in her own ability, but there was more to it than just that.

It felt like she didn't want to ask someone for help.

"But...I guess it's fine..."

It was better to ask my teacher for help, but I also didn't want to get on Sophie's bad side by pestering her too much about it. She was a world-renowned witch, so I figured it would be all right. She was certainly more well-versed both academically and magically than I was.

So I decided to shut away the strange feelings I had.

With that, on the night before the festival, we finished the seventh and final formula that went into creating the portal. All that was left was waiting for the ceremony to start at nine o'clock the next day.

At this point, it was already major news that Sophie would oversee that year's festival, and she was well received by the entire town for it. She didn't need to dye her hair to hide her identity anymore.

"Heh, here, Sophie. I bought you a croquette."

"I'll eat it."

We both ate croquettes as we walked through the town under the setting sun. The road was dyed a crimson orange, which was the same color it turned every night, but it felt different that day. The decorations for the festival were all up, and there was a celebratory mood already spreading throughout the town.

I turned to find Sophie looking like a squirrel as she munched on her croquette.

"Shere ahre a loht of peehple ouht tohnig."

"Please swallow your food before you speak."

"There are a lot of people out tonight."

"Yeah, it's the night before the festival."

This event, which happened once every year, not only helped develop Lapis but also provided much grace for the other worlds. It was the biggest event that happened all year in Lapis and drew in many travelers from around the world.

"So what do you think of the town the night before the big day?"

"I don't hate it."

"That's nice to hear."

There was something warm and kind about the way Sophie watched as people went by. She looked completely different than she had on the first day, when she mentioned wanting to remove magic from the world.

"You like people, don't you?"

"What makes you say that?"

"I just thought you hated them."
"I never said that."
"But you want to get rid of magic, right?"
"I hate magic. But it is the only thing that makes me feel needed."
"Then wouldn't it be scary to lose that? You would lose your place."
Sophie turned and looked me straight in the eyes after I said this.
"Did Faust tell you?"
"Yeah, kind of."
"She's a blabbermouth, then."
"So you aren't denying it… I bet you actually like magic. I love it. I like being a part of this festival, getting to meet you, and when people around town talk to me. I think it's all thanks to magic, and I think the same goes for you, too. That you owe a lot of what you have to magic."
"I don't know."
Sophie looked up at the sky. It had shades of both the day and night sky in it, and the moon was visible.
"You don't have to fit in to the place you were born, you know. If you ever feel lonely, you're always welcome to come here. We can open a circus and have people buy tickets to come see you. It'll be the biggest show on earth—and I'll take a fifty percent cut."
"Spberry."
"Yes?"
"Don't make me hurt you."
Sophie smiled as she said this—she was happy on the inside.

○

It was time to open the portal. We assembled at the large town square in the middle of Lapis. Sophie and I stood within a fenced-off area, a circle with a radius of about twenty meters. Sophie handled the main formula, and I would support her in opening and stabilizing the portal. This was something my teacher always did on her own, but I was going to help this time.

Many people gathered outside the fenced-off area to watch Sophie. There were way more people this year than there usually were. It occurred to me that this was the world Sophie Hayter lived in.

"Okay, Miss Raspberry. We anticipate a bang-up job this year, as you always do."

I shook hands with Mayor Carter. He was a large-framed bearded man I knew well.

"You got it! We're gonna open a portal so grand, it'll turn into a problem with all the noise and trash left behind by the festival. You're going to have to work double time to figure it out after everything's said and done."

"Okay, let's not make it *that* grand."

After the mayor finished shaking my hand, he looked a bit more nervous and did the same for Sophie. With the same resolute expression she always had, she shook his hand.

"S-Sophie Highter. I've heard all about you."

"No."

Sophie shook her head, and the mayor ended up losing face a bit when he let a dumb-sounding "Erm" out.

"Mayor! Her name is Sophie *Hayter*, not whatever you said! It's a big honor she's here; you should at least get her name right."

"Oof, my mistake, Meg."

"Don't apologize to me! Also, you need to call me Miss Raspberry in public!"

"Oh, I, uh..."

The mayor was a mess. Despite his large frame, he looked so small next to Sophie on the stage. Perhaps he was out of his element having to hold this ceremony without my teacher. Whatever the case may have been, it was hard to watch our countryside mayor make a fool of himself in such a public way.

"I think that's enough, Mr. Mayor! How about you stand over there so we can finish up this portal now, okay?"

"Y-yes!"

We watched as he scrambled off the stage, and that was that. My eyes met Sophie's, and it was time.

"Are you ready, Spberry?"

"You bet your bottom dollar I am!"

"What century is that response from?"

While Sophie poked fun at me, she also activated the first magic formula. Despite the sun being up, the immediate vicinity grew dark—a sign the magic was taking effect.

Time and space in the center of the town square began to warp. Sophie then activated both formulas two and three, which created the portal in a single flash, connecting this world with the others.

Though she was moving quickly through the steps, it wasn't too difficult to keep up. This was because my teacher always activated all seven at once. I usually didn't play a part in the ceremony like I was this time, though. I needed to support Sophie, who was using this spell for the first time in her life, using the knowledge and experience I had from watching my teacher all these years. I should have been able to emulate my teacher, if not just by a smidgen.

I would set off the fourth and fifth formulas, which stabilized the portal and helped it take hold in our world. All that was left was using the sixth formula to formulate the physical portal, then the seventh to add a barrier for safety.

I watched as Sophie activated the sixth formula, which constructed the portal, and something suddenly caught my eye. It was the seventh formula Sophie had ready—there was a kink in its form.

"Sophie, wait!"

"...?"

As I said this, the seventh formula began to fall apart. A bright line shone out for a brief instant before the seventh formula disappeared, and the barrier vanished into thin air. This triggered a big shock wave, which caused Sophie and me both to fall where we stood.

It all happened in an instant.

"Ow..."

I sat up, and what I saw shocked me.

Evidently, the crowd had no idea that this was a problem, and so they were cheering for the portal that opened up.

It was only Sophie and I who knew what happened.

○

The portal to the other worlds. On the other end of the portal were thousands upon thousands of other worlds. There were worlds that sought to cultivate prosperity with our own, and conversely, worlds that only brought chaos.

Intermingling with other worlds helped to advance our own and was a catalyst for this world's cultural evolution. This made it possible to achieve many advancements in agriculture, manufacturing, and architecture. There were, of course, also cases of our world sharing techniques and technologies with other worlds as well.

The role the portal played was to bring about the greatest good for citizens of all worlds who passed through it. It wasn't all roses, though. Throughout the long history of this tradition, there were isolated cases where the portal triggered a disaster. This included the spread of new germs, such as black blood disease and monera fever—illnesses that were said to have been brought to this world through the portal. These diseases resulted in the deaths of thousands, and it took nearly fifty years to find cures.

Magical beasts finding their way through the portal also caused the deaths of hundreds before eventually being eradicated. There was also a case where the mage ended up getting eaten alive by what passed through, too.

The portal, while a beacon of prosperity, also harbored the potential for tremendous danger. This was what the barrier was for—to keep any dangers from finding their way through the portal into our world.

It was arguably the most important part of the spell, and it had failed, with the portal up and running in full. This meant there was a possibility that everyone at the town square could be in grave danger.

This is bad, this is bad, this is bad, this is bad...

There was an alarm going off in my mind. My entire body was covered in a cold sweat, and my heart was pumping so hard that it made me feel dizzy.

I needed to figure out exactly what had happened and act fast. If we screwed this up, this day could go down in history as a bloody massacre.

We need to move...!

"Sophie!"

I yelled out her name, and she snapped back to reality and looked at me.

"Create a new barrier! I will buy us the time we need!"

While Sophie drew up the massive spell formula for the barrier from scratch, I needed to act fast to throw up a temporary one. Drawing it out on the ground would take way too long—I needed to make the barrier appear as soon as possible.

I found myself recalling the conversation Sophie and I had the day before.

* * *

"How do you draw out formulas with your hand like that?"

"...It takes two steps. First, you bring your magic to your fingertip to give it the same effect as chanting. Then you release that magic to create a flow that makes up the formula. Executing these two steps in as little time as possible also serves to shorten the casting process."

I collected my magical energy into my finger and imagined the flow of the magic circle in my mind. With the magic circle inside me, I then used my fingertip as an exit for it to take effect. That was what I pictured, at least.

Was it going to work? I had no way of knowing and was about to find out.

With my magic in my finger, I pointed to draw through the air, and I could feel something strange. It was a feeling I felt for the first time in my entire life, like I was pressing my finger against an invisible acrylic board.

This is it... I can do this...!

I began spelling out the first character, and a line made of light illuminated behind my finger. I wrote out a simplified version of the spell and activated it. I could then see the barrier being formed before my very eyes.

It worked...!

I didn't have time to get excited over pulling off a technique for the first time. It was easy to throw up a simple barrier, but they only lasted around ten seconds at most. I needed to get the next one going as soon as I finished the first.

One barrier, two barriers, three barriers, four.

One after another, I produced the barrier spells. I needed to avoid focusing too much on how I was doing it in the first place and somehow ignore the immense pressure under which I felt like I could faint at any given moment.

There was so much I had to process in my mind that my nose

started bleeding. I ignored it, though, and kept throwing up more barriers as the previous ones dissipated.

I knew if I failed here, I would regret it for the rest of my life.

Faster, faster! I need to run through the formula faster.

I could feel myself making the barriers even faster. At the same time, I could feel the intense toll it was taking on my body. I'd never used so much magic in such quick succession before.

"Faster… Faster…"

My mind was beginning to go blank. Slowly, my vision grew dark starting from the outer edges, and my thoughts grew clouded.

How long have I been casting for? How many barriers did I manage to make…?

I soon woke up to someone grabbing my hand.

"Spberry. You did good."

"Sophie…"

"Everything is all right now."

Hearing her say this, I noticed that the barrier had been cast around the portal. Not only was it up, it was also fortified. The formula used for its magic circle had been redesigned and improved.

"How long have I been out…?"

"For about two or three minutes."

"That's all?"

Sophie managed to not only re-create but improve the barrier formula in a matter of minutes? She may have messed up, but wow, did she know how to make a comeback. They didn't call her a genius for nothing.

"Wow, you Sages sure are something else, eh?"

"Your nose is bleeding, Spberry."

"Oh, you're right."

"One more thing."

"Hmm?"

"Thank you."

Sophie didn't look at me when she said this. I could tell she was blushing as she did, though.

I got up, and we bowed for the audience, who gave us a grand round of applause. Sophie, who was used to putting on a show, waved for the spectators. She really was a celebrity. It made her feel so far away, even though she was right next to me.

With that, the Celebration of Worlds began.

○

"What?! You made a mistake creating the magic formula?"

"Yeah, ha-ha. Sorry."

I scratched my head, and Mayor Carter looked terrified as he uttered, "Meg…"

After we finished the opening ceremony, we went to the town hall to tell the mayor what had happened. Sophie and I stood opposite his desk as we told him the news.

"Will there be any side effects from this?"

"No, everything should be fine."

Sophie quietly nodded as she said this.

"I've heard of major accidents happening related to portals in the past…"

"Past incidents were always the result of a delayed response, with the problem being left undiscovered for days at a time. There won't be any issues with a three-minute opening at most."

"Well, that's a relief…"

Something dawned on me as I listened to the explanation.

"Wait… You don't mean to say I panicked for no reason, do you?"

"That is what this would mean. We wouldn't hold such a dangerous event publicly every year, would we?"

"Well, yeah, but why didn't you say something sooner?! So you mean to say you let a beautiful damsel show her bloody face in front of the entire town for nothing?! I even stuffed a tissue up my nose…"

"Yeah, that was really funny. I think the townsfolk enjoyed it, too."

"It's all right, Meg. It was a good show, and that's what counts."

"You're not helping, Mayor!"

Bickering about it only made me even more tired. I let out a sigh and almost lost my footing, but I managed to put my hand on the desk to catch myself. This worried the mayor, who was watching.

"Are you all right? You don't seem well."

"Yeah… I haven't felt so hot ever since the portal ceremony. I feel drained."

"That is what happens when you use spells rapid-fire like that. It takes getting used to, forming magic formulas inside yourself."

"Is that right? I'll be sure to eat some liver later, then."

"Why liver?"

"I figured it would help get my blood flowing better."

"The hematopoietic mechanism responsible for the proliferation of your blood vessels exhibits no discernible relationship with magic energy restoration."

"We speak English here…"

As Sophie and I poked fun at each other, the mayor interjected with "But… The last thing I expected with the presence of one of the Seven Sages was a magical error. I suppose mistakes happen, though."

"I…"

"Oh, it was my fault. I'm sorry."

Sophie gave me a surprised look as I said this. I gave her a wink to tell her I would handle it with the mayor.

"Well, things worked out this time, so all is well. But you ought to be careful. You wouldn't want to tarnish your teacher's name as well."

"Yeah, you're right."

"I'll let Lady Faust know about this."

"Okay..."

Am I gonna be okay? My teacher might make me work for three days and nights without sleep. Or maybe something even worse, like making me climb a mountain during the winter with no clothes as some form of ascetic training?

"Ah-ha-ha... Perhaps death is the only true release. All things eventually perish, and any pain or embarrassment is less than a mosquito bite in the grand scheme of the universe. That's right, life is a test. As my wise, ascended teacher once showed me. The purpose of life is to find your twin flame..."

"Are you all right, Meg?"

"Just feeling a bit worried is all."

I could only imagine the horrors that awaited me as Sophie and I excused ourselves from the mayor's office. With my shoulders slumped, I meandered out of the town hall, and Sophie followed a few paces behind.

"Spberry."

"Yes?"

"Why did you lie?"

"Lie? About what?"

"About making the mistake..."

"I mean, it was my fault for not looking into it enough beforehand and realizing the formula was changed. More importantly, though, there are much fewer repercussions for some apprentice like me to mess up than there are one of the Seven Sages, right?"

It was a mistake that could have led to Sophie, a Sage, causing a big accident at a small-town event. If word got out about it, it would be a scandal of epic proportions. It could even lead to her losing her seat as one of the Seven Sages.

"I'm used to it anyway. I'm always messing up."

"But…"

"It's easier this way. A Sage covered for a witch in training to stop a big accident. And…"

"And…?"

"I know you were only trying to make the festival better for the town anyway. I didn't want Lapis to be a town you remembered for something negative."

"Spberry…"

"Now let's get back. The festivities have already started."

I grabbed Sophie's hand, and she squeezed mine back. She did so with a hint of hesitation—in a way two lovers who weren't sure of how strong they should hold each other's hands did.

"Wow, you purty girls have some real soft hands on ya."

"Let go of me."

"But I won't do that."

I continued to hold her hand and drag her out of the building. Once we were out, I could see the surprise on her face. She gazed at the town, which was lively with people celebrating and enjoying the festival. There were colorful flags all around and pop-up shops lining the street—it was like Lapis had transformed overnight.

"You helped make this possible, Miss Sophie. You brought all these people happiness, but I'm sure you're used to doing that by now."

"Yes, but…it's my first time actually being able to take it in like this. Usually, I have to move on to my next job once I'm finished with my part of the show."

Sophie looked happy as she gazed at the town.

"Let's go check out the food stalls, Miss Sophie. You in the mood for anything in particular?

"It's Sophie."

"Huh?"

"I'd prefer you just call me Sophie."

Sophie gave me a genuine smile as she said this. So genuine that I nearly choked.

She was the witch who captivated the world, and I got to see her real smile.

"You're even more beautiful when you smile…"

"You have a bad habit of sounding like a creepy old guy, Spberry."

"Who you's callin' a guy, lady?"

Sophie grabbed my hand this time. It caught me off guard at first, but it made me happy from the bottom of my heart.

"Let's go, Sophie!" I called out to her, my voice becoming a part of the festivities that rang out in the bright blue sky that day.

Chapter 6:
Flowers
Blossom in
the Festival's
Night Sky

"Meg."
"Oh, uh, yes?"
"Your spell failed."
"Mm…"
Later that night, my teacher was waiting for me in the study when I got home.
"I heard you flubbed your part of the barrier's construction."
"Yes… I'm really sorry. My only request is that if you're going to kill me over it, please feed my body to my two familiars."
My pair of familiars shuddered at the thought, but my teacher quickly dispelled their concerns by following with "Calm yourself. I have no intent of reprimanding you over it. You did it to protect Sophie, yes?"
My teacher looked straight into my eyes as she said this, and I could tell she knew everything. There was no way to pull the wool over the Eternal Witch's All-Seeing Eye.
"While that may be the case, any more flops will certainly tarnish your name as a witch. I suppose it isn't a problem if you are okay with nobody taking you seriously."
"Tsk, tsk, tsk, Teacher. You're a hundred million years too young if you don't think I'll spring back from this."
"You're in no place to be making jokes with only ten months left to live. Seeing as your dignity is on the line, I've decided to give you another job to handle."
"A job?"
"You are to be in the parade."

"What parade…?"

"The parade being held for the Celebration of Worlds. When the mayor heard Sophie would be coming to Lapis, he requested that she hold a parade during her stay. You will act as her assistant once more to help her with the parade."

It made a lot of sense. Why not throw a parade when the world's best parade thrower was in town? I couldn't blame the mayor for wanting my teacher to make it happen.

That said, I was a bit anxious about taking on the role.

"I mean, I'm all for un-tarnishing my name and all, but…do you think it will fly with the mayor? I doubt he'll trust a witch who screwed up as much as I did."

"We'll tell him that I am the one who wants you to assist me." Sophie was standing in the doorway. "That I won't hold a parade unless it's Spberry helping me."

"Sophie…"

"There you have it. Sophie is one of the Seven Sages with duties outside the parade, as am I. It is better for us to have assistance from where we can get it. I'll let the mayor know that I'll take care of whatever happens if things go awry. Also, my back is feeling much better thanks to your herbal patch."

"You'd do all that for me?"

"Your name being tarnished tarnishes mine as well."

"You adults and your silly names." Something then crossed my mind. "But wait, don't we hold a fireworks show every year for the festival? If we hold a parade, won't it put a damper on the fireworks show?"

"Unfortunately, there won't be a fireworks show this year."

"Why's that?"

"The town's amazing fireworks maker passed away this year from an illness."

"What…?"

I'd never met the fireworks maker before, but his creations were something I looked forward to every year. Hearing that he'd passed away was quite shocking.

"That is why it falls on you and Sophie to lift the town's spirits for the festival."

"Are you okay with this, Sophie?"

"I'm the one who caused trouble in the first place, and I don't like owing anyone favors. I won't let things end this way. I will get my revenge."

"What was that last part?"

"Then it's settled. I will be leaving this to you."

My teacher looked at me with her usual grin, which gave me the confidence to answer with a bold "You've got it!"

○

Lapis was always lively in the days leading up to the Celebration of Worlds. The entire town was filled with guests from other worlds. Beastfolk, elves, dwarves, and any other mythical creature imaginable. These guests who came from beyond the portal were referred to as our otherworldly neighbors.

There weren't many opportunities for different worlds to connect, as the number of locations that could magically support an open portal were limited in both this world and others, making the Celebration of Worlds a special event. This was why so many guests came from such a wide variety of worlds. This was also what made Lapis's Celebration of Worlds so famous.

Travelers who saw otherworldly neighbors walk the streets of Lapis were often captivated by the sight; some even took out their phones to snap photos. The citizens of Lapis, however, were more accustomed to the annual visit, with many of them approaching the guests for conversation.

Most of the drifters who found their way to our world were good people. At the very least, the barrier kept anyone who harbored ill will from passing through.

I walked down the main street, taking in the lively air of peace that could be felt throughout Lapis. Next to me was a brown-haired girl with a hat and glasses. It was Sophie, in disguise.

"Okay, Sophie. I want you to teach me everything you know about parade throwing."

"I will, in exchange for a sample of all the morsels available at the stands today."

"Riiight." I didn't have the money for that. I would have to send the mayor an invoice for it later. "But wow, just look at all the people."

"Is it rare for it to be this crowded?"

"You betcha. This is a small town, after all. Don't get me wrong, it gets crowded around this time every year, but there's way more people here than usual. And they're here to see you and the parade we're going to hold. It's fun just thinking about showing all these people our parade."

"You seem happy, Spberry."

"It's not every day you get to throw a parade. I'm also excited to see how many tears of joy this rakes in for me."

This was it. Holding an event that moved people to tears meant more tears in my pocket. It was my big chance, maybe even my only one, and it definitely helped that I had Sophie, one of the Seven Sages, in my camp.

Sophie frowned at my remark.

"What are you going to do with tears of joy?"

"Huh?"

Thinking back on it, I'd never had the chance to talk about my curse with Sophie—to explain that if nothing was done, I would die in ten months. After telling a handful of friends about this, I thought it would be easier to talk about by now.

"Well, the thing is…"

I couldn't find the right words to break it to her.

"Spberry."

"Yes!"

"The food on that stand looks delicious."

"Huh? Oh, the skewer place…?"

The tension released from my shoulders when Sophie decided to abruptly change the subject. We were about to pass a stand that was serving food from another country.

Sophie, drawn by the smell, began slowly veering toward the shop front. She was like an animal.

"I want to eat here."

"You're free to buy a skewer, if you'd like."

"I don't have any cash."

"But you're a Sage?"

"I put everything on my card."

"You're so bougie…"

I trailed behind Sophie, staring at her back. I wondered what she would think if she learned that her new friend was going to die soon.

I couldn't bring myself to say it yet, and as we continued to explore the different stands set up all around the main street, the subject of our conversation drifted to something entirely different.

We were supposed to be there to get a lay of the street for the parade, but Sophie was having too much fun. She had almost more food than she could carry, which she stuffed into her expressionless face—looking like an apathetic hamster. She was definitely enjoying herself, to say the least.

"Do you not get the chance to come to these events often?"

"*Om nom nom.* Ah do buh *nom nom.*"

"Please swallow your food before you try to speak."

"I do, but never at a leisurely pace like we are today."

"That's a surprise, considering you attend some of the world's largest festivals."

"If people find out I'm there, it draws a crowd. Plus, it would be boring to come to one of these alone."

Oh, she's usually the main attraction at events like this. People would definitely want to approach her if they saw her walking around on the street alone, which must make it difficult to go out by herself.

"I guess that makes me, the first person you've gone to a festival with, your first friend."

"The concept of a friend feels vague to me. And you're my assistant."

"You're cruisin' for a bruisin'."

Lapis looked like a different town during the Celebration of Worlds. A few steps down the main road and you would pass by a kobold, a dwarf sharing stories over some ale, and an elf getting hit on—and not being totally turned off by it. There were young people, likely from far away, who dressed up for the event, and there were decorations all over town. It almost felt like a second Halloween. The only difference was that they weren't wearing costumes.

We were wading our way through the crowded street when Sophie suddenly turned to me and said, "I'm starting to get tired," then sighed.

"Do you want to go rest somewhere? I'd like to sit and eat the food we've bought."

"Yes, let's do that."

"I think there was a hotel near here."

"Why a hotel?"

"You know what I'm talkin' 'bout, baby."

"Creep."

After she said this, Sophie grabbed my hand and pulled me

into an alleyway. My heart started racing. *She isn't really going to take me to a hotel, is she?*

"Who's trying to bring who to a hotel again…?"

"Quiet."

I was confused, but after passing through a few streets, we emerged into an open space. It was behind a building but had a nice bench in the sun where we could park ourselves. I'd never been to this spot before.

"I stumbled upon this place the other day."

"Wow, I didn't even know there was a place like this here."

There was hardly anybody around, save for a woman sitting alone on the bench. It was a big bench, and she would probably let us use it if we asked.

"Is this seat open?"

"Yes. Please, go ahead."

She was a beautiful, mature-looking woman with a cardigan draped across her shoulders. Her hair was blond and tied up; it shone beautifully in the sun.

At some point during my momentary infatuation with the woman's looks, Sophie had already sat on the bench. I took the only open spot left, which ended up being between Sophie and the woman. On top of that, Sophie started chowing down on the food we bought from the stands before I could even catch my breath.

"Sophie, please try to eat your food more slowly."

"Nom nom. Munch, munch."

Despite her dainty looks, Sophie had quite the stomach on her. I must've looked like an animal tamer unable to gain control over her beast, because the woman sitting next to us chuckled under her breath.

"You two are funny."

"Oh, sorry. I hope we're not bothering you."

"No, it's fine. It was too quiet here anyway."

"What are you doing here, sitting on a bench all by yourself?"

"I'm waiting for someone."

"Oh? A friend?"

"Yes… A friend I made here one year ago."

The woman introduced herself as Marie, and she told us about how she came here to meet a man she'd met at the last Celebration of Worlds.

Marie shared with us what happened on the night of the Celebration of Worlds when she escaped the crowd after a sudden onset of nausea.

"I don't feel well. Maybe it's the crowd."

She looked around for a place to sit but wasn't able to find any free benches or chairs due to the number of people there for the event. When she almost fell over, a man appeared and helped her find her footing.

"Are you all right?" he'd asked.

The man wore a heavy mountain jacket with a hood. Because it was nighttime, it was too dark to make out his face, but she found something comforting about his large frame.

"Thank you. I'm just feeling a little dizzy."

"There's a bench over there. Maybe you should have a seat."

Though his unique outfit initially made Marie feel a bit uncomfortable, it was clear the man harbored no bad intentions. Soon enough, she found herself trusting him. He seemed like a good person.

The man led Marie to a bench—the very one where we sat today. He gently lowered her onto the bench before going to buy a mineral water somewhere nearby. Afterward, he stayed by her side as she recuperated. Marie's dizziness soon faded, and she realized it had probably been due to her low blood pressure.

As she recovered, the man tried to keep her spirits up by sharing tales of a distant land. He was a stranger, a person from a world with unfamiliar customs. Yet it didn't take long for Marie to find herself captivated by his stories and unique personality.

"You're a really nice person. What country are you from?"

"I'm—"

Just as he was about to speak, some fireworks burst in the sky. It was a beautiful show of fiery lights, illuminating the sky for all to see and capturing both Marie's and the man's attention.

"Sure is beautiful..."

"I'm glad I got to see it again."

"Again?"

"I come here every year for the fireworks."

The two continued watching the fireworks show together before the man eventually stood and told Marie that he needed to go.

"I really enjoyed speaking with you and ended up staying here for a bit too long."

"Will I ever see you again?"

"Maybe, if our paths cross."

Without being able to properly thank the man, she watched as he disappeared into the crowd.

"Wow, how romantic. So you're here to meet him again."

"Yes. I thought he might come back to this spot."

"You haven't seen him since?"

"Not once. He seemed like a traveler, so my best guess is that he's out exploring the world. That said, I always come here with the hope that he might show up again. He did say he loved this town's fireworks, after all. I figured the Celebration of Worlds would be my best chance to meet him again."

"Is that right? But wait, I heard the fireworks maker passed away this year..."

"What...?"

Marie's eyes widened for a moment, only to revert to her usual expression. She looked down and murmured, "Oh... I thought maybe I could meet him again during the fireworks show, but... Well, I guess our paths just weren't meant to cross."

Marie's shoulders slumped. She stood and softly said, "I need to go now. I appreciate you listening to my story. Your company helped cheer me up."

"Are you sure you want to give up now, Marie? You love that man, don't you?"

"I don't know. I just think about that day we spent together. He was someone I met randomly, though. I always figured I'd probably never see him again."

"But what if he's *the one*? It's not every day you fall head over heels for someone, after all. I'd keep trying if I were you. Right, Sophie?"

I looked over to Sophie, who was more focused on devouring her last skewer than the conversation at hand. She'd gone through pretty much all the food she'd bought.

"What the—?! You ate my food, too!"

"Munch, munch. Crunch, crunch."

"Don't think you can chew your way out of this one! I'll open up that little mouth and clean it out with a kiss if I have to! Pucker up!"

I was grabbing on to Sophie's collar and shaking her at this point but was interrupted by Marie's giggles.

"Heh-heh... Sorry, you two are just so funny."

"Here's an idea, Marie. How about we meet up here tomorrow? I'll bring the man you're looking for if I find him. And you can give up after that if you want."

"Sure, I suppose," Marie said with a nod. Her smile was faint, with a hint of loneliness to it.

"I hope I didn't say something I shouldn't have...," I muttered as Sophie and I watched Marie walk away.

Sophie nodded.

"The man she's looking for may not even be in town. I think letting her give up would've been kinder."

"But you heard her; he made it sound like he comes every year."

"If he only came here for the fireworks, there's a good chance he checks the schedule to see if there will be any before coming. It's written on the city's event page that they won't be holding the show this year."

"Yeah, but still..."

Something told me it was a bit too early to give up. I wasn't going to give a spiel about fate and destiny, but something about a person waiting an entire year just for a chance to meet someone seemed special to me.

The two of us returned to the parade route, this time heading toward where the parade would exit the town. We thought about what sort of spectacles we'd create in different parts of the town, and I let Sophie know which spots would have the best vantage points and what sort of architecture to bear in mind.

It was crowded throughout the entire stretch of town we were going to use, and as we moved away from its center, more creatures joined in on the mix, such as gargantuan titans and what looked like humans but were actually cyclops. The Celebration of Worlds could be felt all over the city.

"It's important to know about the venue for big shows."

"Really?"

"You need to think about how the magic will look to the audience and what you can do to make it easier to take in. To be a pro is to always have your audience in mind. I need to be able to select from multiple patterns to answer what best matches the crowd on the day of the parade."

"Uh-huh."

"Spberry… Are you listening?"

"Sure, sure."

My empty responses must've ticked off Sophie, because she karate-chopped my rib cage, which made me yelp in pain.

"What are you so distracted by?"

"Oh, you know. Maybe if I keep my eyes peeled, I can find Marie's love interest."

"Even if he's here, he might not be wearing the same jacket she told us about. There are countless big men in mountain jackets out here today."

"That's true."

"You should stop trying to do something so pointless."

"We won't know if it's pointless until we try, though." As I talked back to Sophie, she abruptly stopped in her tracks. "What's up?"

"That…"

Sophie pointed to the crowd, and standing a head above everyone else was a large man in an orange mountain jacket, carrying a big backpack. He had his hood on and was walking through the busy street.

Wait, is that actually him?
Maybe?
You know, I think it is.
It definitely is.
If that ain't him, then he ain't here!

A meeting of multiple tiny Meg Raspberrys convened in my mind, reaching a unanimous decision. Despite my certainty, I had no concrete proof. It just seemed too coincidental for someone who perfectly matched the description to appear like this.

This is fate.

"Follow that man, Sophie!"

As soon as I spoke, we sprang into action, trailing the man. Unfortunately, the dense crowd had other plans, making it nearly impossible for us to push through. At this rate, we were going to lose him.

"How about this?!"

I scrambled up a stone wall bordering the street and perched on top. The passersby all turned to stare as I extended my arm, pointing directly at the man in the bulky orange jacket.

"You, sir, in the big orange jacket! Stop right there!"

Startled by my booming voice, the man looked over, then began to run away.

"Hey! Where do you think you're going? Come back here!"

I took off along the stone wall, giving chase. My sense of balance was excellent, and I had always been more physically fit than magically skilled. I was determined not to let him escape.

Noticing my balancing act on top of the wall, the man cut through the crowd and emerged into an empty alleyway. I was going to need to cross the road if I was going to catch him now.

"Not so fast, backpack boy!"

I focused my magic into my finger and wrote a formula onto my feet that allowed me to ignore gravity. I used Sophie's method to cast my magic circle. Using a formula in my mind, I actualized it with my hands. This was something I'd figured out how to do during the Portal Ceremony.

My body became weightless. With a leap of faith, I soared over the crowd, floating through the air. I maintained my momentum until I reached the opposite end of the street, where I canceled my spell and landed firmly on the ground.

"Wait up!"

Watching the poor man flee for his life, I broke into a full-body sprint, fixated on his back. I gracefully leaped over a toppled trashcan in the alleyway and dodged a waltzing tabby cat. I was completely in the zone.

The only problem was that this alleyway led to another main road. If he reached it before me, I might lose him for good. As I racked my brain for a solution, I realized we were nearing a wall.

A wall? When did they build that?

Unaware of my confusion, the man ran down the alley, the one with a dead end.

Just as I suspected, the man was trapped with no escape route. Breathing heavily, I wiped some drool from my mouth as I closed in.

"*Huff*... *Huff*... Geh-heh-heh... I have you now."

His back was against the wall. I slowly advanced toward him, only to be snapped out of my hunter's trance by a voice behind me. "Spberry."

"Sophie! Where were you?"

"I went around and set up an illusionary wall."

"Oh."

"It would've been easier to catch him if you weren't chasing him like that."

"Oh."

This revelation solved the mystery of the random wall; it was Sophie's creation. But when and how did she manage to get ahead of us?

You Seven Sages are built different, aren'cha?

The man, clearly shaken and looking out of place with his imposing figure, stared at us.

"Wh-who are you two?"

"You's got nothing to worry about, see? Just come here with us for a bit, see?"

"I-I'd really rather not..."

"Lookie here, Sophie. We's got ourselves a wise guy. Let's see how tough he is without the hood!"

Reaching out, I removed the man's hood and revealed his identity—leaving both me and Sophie utterly speechless.

"Don't look at me!"

"You..."

His face was covered in fluffy fur, with a long snout and sharp eyes.

He was a wolfman.

○

"I was hiding my face because I didn't want anyone to find out..."

Once things had calmed down, we brought the wolfman to the side of the road, where he quietly confided in us. The reason he hid his face and identity was because he didn't want anyone to know he was from another world.

"Why would you want to hide your face? There are all sorts of people from all over the worlds here today. I mean, we passed a kobold, an elf, and a lizardman just while we were chasing you."

"I've been coming to this town ever since I was little, but one time, some of the townsfolk thought I was a real wolf. I do this so I don't scare them."

"So that's why you ran away from us?"

"Well, no... I ran away from you out of fear, due to the bloodthirsty look in your eyes."

"Was I really that scary...?"

I turned to Sophie, who quietly confirmed with a nod.

"You had the eyes of a predator staring down its prey. The eyes of a killer."

"That's odd. I'd intended to show a smile of love and mercy."

"Maybe you should hold those emotions back. It was quite horrifying."

"You really should keep some comments to yourself..."

"So why were you two trying to get my attention?"

Oh yeah. I'd almost forgotten the reason we'd chased him down in the first place.

"We actually have a friend who's been looking for you."

"For me...?"

"That being said, we had no way of knowing it was you without talking to you. Do you remember helping a young woman during last year's Celebration of Worlds?"

"Ah..."

The wolfman reacted to that. I turned to Sophie; it looked like we had our guy.

"Does that sound familiar to you?"

"I helped out a girl who was feeling sick last year. We had a chat and watched the fireworks together."

"The person you helped is looking for you."

"Why's that...?"

"Well, that should be obvious. Because she wants to see you again. She's never forgotten about you."

"Really? That girl..." The wolfman brightened for a moment, but then he shook his head as if to shake himself back to reality and quietly murmured, "I can't. I can't meet her. I know she'll be disappointed to find out the person she's been wanting to see all this time is some hideous wolf."

"Why would she..."

...think that? I couldn't bring myself to finish my sentence. It was true—a small portion of the population found people from other worlds scary.

"It's for the best."

"But is it best for you?"

"What...?"

"It sounds to me like you haven't forgotten about her, either. Just now, you looked pretty excited for a split second."

The wolfman's expression darkened.

"I mean, I thought she seemed like a wonderful, mature, gentle person. I'd like to meet up and chat with her again, if I could."

"Then why not now that you can? Why give up?"

"It's better this way."

"No it isn't!"

I ended up yelling at the man, which surprised both him and Sophie. I continued, though, poking his chest with my finger.

"Why is everyone so willing to give up?! 'Oh, it might not work'—you won't know until you try! You were the one who approached her last year! And she liked the time she spent with you! And now you have a chance to meet her again! So why toss it away 'cause you're anxious?!"

"That's easy to say, but..."

"Fine! How about this? I'll tell her we found you, but you're a wolfman. If she...Marie says yes, will you agree to meet up with her?"

"Marie?"

"That's her name."

"So her name was Marie..."

The wolfman's gloomy expression brightened once more with a warm smile. It was clear he had feelings for Marie, even if he denied it.

"Did you know they aren't having the fireworks show this year?"

"Yes, I heard the townspeople speaking about it. I heard the fireworks maker passed away."

"That's right. Marie told us you came here for the fireworks. Is she right?"

"Yes, she is."

"So despite there being no fireworks, you're still here. I'd wager it's because you'd like to see Marie again, isn't it?"

The wolfman fidgeted as I said this, indicating my guess was likely correct.

"You don't have to reply to my offer right now, but take some time to think about it, Mr. Wolfman."

"It's Wuf."

"Huh?"

"Wuf Shin. That's my name."

"Wuf Shin. Got it. That's a strange name."

"It's not strange in my world."

"Spberry has a strange name even for our world."

"You're the only one who calls me that!"

After a brief rest, we collected our thoughts and continued.

"So are we all good, Wuf Shin? Remember, you don't need to accept my offer yet."

"Yeah, that sounds fine," Wuf said with a bright youthful expression. He gave off an entirely different feel from the tired old dog he looked like before.

"By the way. How old are you?"

"Me? I'm twenty-five."

"Twenty-five…"

Doesn't that make him well over one hundred in dog years? I wonder how wolfman years are different.

We decided to meet up there again before going our separate ways with Wuf.

"You sure we shouldn't ask him for his contact information?" Sophie asked as we watched him go.

"I mean, I doubt someone from another world has a phone or computer."

"That's not the case, according to recent reports. There are people who become pen pals with those in other worlds via e-mail."

"Really? Wow…"

So modern technology is becoming interdimensional technology? I guess if it's the same service provider and internet, then maybe…? How's that supposed to work…?

"Either way, we have a time and place where we're gonna meet up, so it should be okay. If he doesn't show, then he doesn't show."

At the end of the day, this was his decision to make and not ours. Wuf and Marie barely knew each other, and a year was a long time for love at first sight to last. I couldn't imagine having long-lasting feelings for someone I'd briefly met during a trip.

But the chance to meet again presented itself, and it was clear they at least had some feelings for each other.

They were worlds apart, in a literal sense, and this went for their races and standings within their own worlds as well. They would each have to overcome these differences of their own accord to come together in the middle.

My role in this was to be a witch-turned-cupid, nothing more, nothing less.

○

I met up with Marie where we planned, and she greeted me by happily jumping up and saying, "There you are! Where's your friend?"

"She, uh, got a bit hung up on something…"

On the way to the meet-up spot, someone saw through Sophie's disguise, and she ended up getting swarmed by fans of the world-famous celebrity. It soon devolved into an impromptu autograph signing event with a police presence watching over the crowd.

"I have two pieces of news for you."

"Is it about him?"

"Yes. Now, I don't want you to be surprised when I tell you this, but…"

I told Marie everything. That Wuf was a wolfman from another world and that he was hesitant to meet Marie again. Marie took it all in and responded with a hushed "That's a relief. I'm just happy to hear he remembered me."

"Aren't you surprised he's a wolfman?"

"Well, yes and no. Honestly, a part of me thought this might be the case. It was the Celebration of Worlds, and he was hiding his face, after all. I figured he could be from another world."

"Is that right...?"

Marie wasn't attracted to him for his looks or due to the romance of their meet-cute, but his personality. Setting aside whether her feelings would turn into something serious, I was relieved to hear this about her.

"So he's not a human man, but are you still willing to meet him?"

"Yes, I am." Marie said this, then continued. "Actually, it wouldn't be my first run-in with a wolfman."

"Oh?"

"It happened a long time ago, when I was a child. I met a young wolfboy who was lost. I walked along with him while we searched for his parents. Thinking back on it, we saw the fireworks together that year, too..."

"What happened to that boy?"

"Somebody thought he was a real wolf, like the animal, and that he was trying to attack me. It caused a big scene, and though I was able to convince everyone I was fine, we were separated in the commotion. That's why when I heard he was a wolfman, it felt like fate, even if he is a different person."

"That is a pretty big coincidence."

Then it hit me—I remembered what Wuf had told me: that he hid his identity because someone thought he was a wolf when he was a kid. Maybe, just maybe...Wuf was the same wolfboy Marie was talking about.

While I tried to decide whether to tell Marie this, I noticed that she was quietly looking up at the sky.

"Tomorrow is the last day of the Celebration of Worlds. It's a shame there will be no fireworks this year."

"Do you want to see them again, too?"

"Yes... The fireworks are special to me, because they remind me of when I met him. It would've been nice to watch them together with him, just one more time."

"I think I can make that happen."

"What do you mean?"

"I mean there will be some fireworks in the sky tomorrow. You can count on it."

The Celebration of Worlds was going to end the next day. It was the day Sophie and I would hold the parade as well.

I couldn't help but think this was what it would have been like to hold a school festival, if I had gone to school. I felt a little sad that it was going to end, like I was about to wake up from a dream.

After I'd left Marie and headed back home, Sophie showed up while I practiced for the next day in the front yard and commented, "You sure seem fired up."

"Oh, you're back already?"

"After a few hours of handshakes and signing things, it feels like my hand is going to fall off."

"Ha-ha-ha, I bet. Welp, all's well that ends well."

"Spberry. You left me there to die. You deserve to be punished."

"Aw, c'mon. I'm sorry."

Sophie and I joked back and forth, and it was clear she wasn't really mad at me. She ended up taking a seat on a stump near where I was practicing.

"What are you doing?" she inquired.

"I'm practicing drawing magic circles with my finger. I almost have the hang of it, but I don't want to slip up during the parade, so I figured I'd practice a little."

"I can cover you if something goes wrong."

"I know, but I need to learn to do it by myself anyway."

It was quiet outside, and there wasn't a cloud in the darkening sky. Seeing as it was warm during the day, it wasn't likely to rain the next day.

"Spberry, I want to ask you something," Sophie said out of nowhere. "What drives you?"

"What do you mean?"

"You're always so busy helping other people."

"You think so?"

"Modern people are less preoccupied with the business of others. It's rather strange, really. I mean you, as a person."

"You don't need to go that far with it."

"Do you do it for the tears of joy, Spberry?"

"Huh?"

With Sophie being as clever as she was, it was clear to her that this remark caught me off guard.

"You know… I…"

It took me a moment to find the right words. I didn't want to lie about it, after all.

"Honestly, the tears are important, but that's not all there is to it." Sophie looked straight into my eyes and listened earnestly to my response. "I just want people near me to be as happy as can be. When people trust me enough to share about themselves and their past, it makes me happy, and I guess I just want to return the favor. If I do something that somehow makes someone else happy…it makes me feel like my life has meaning to it. I hope that doesn't sound too overexaggerated."

"It doesn't. There's something else I really want to know, too. Why are you collecting tears of joy in the first place?"

"Can that...wait till tomorrow?"

"I need to know. It's eating away at me. I haven't had a full night's sleep because of it. It could ruin the parade tomorrow, which would tarnish my name. I'd be dropped as one of the Seven Sages, and it'd be all your fault."

"I didn't realize you had the mental fortitude of a wet paper towel..."

I could tell Sophie was serious—she was practically threatening me. It didn't look like I could wiggle my way out of this one. Not that I was hiding it in the first place. In fact, I had intended to tell her either way, but I hadn't found the right time yet. I wanted to wait until after everything was over...after the parade the next day.

Sophie, however, was dead set on this. I could see it in her eyes, and I knew now was the time.

"The thing is, I only have one year left to live. Well, ten months, to be precise."

I decided to tell her, and her wide eyes made her shock apparent. It was the most expression I'd ever seen on her usually emotionless face.

"On my seventeenth birthday, my teacher told me I have exactly one year left to live and that the only way I could survive was by using the tears."

"You're going to use a seed of life to extend your life...?"

"You Seven Sages really know your stuff, eh?"

I cracked a joke, but her expression remained the same. Her gaze quavered with compassion and sadness; I could tell she felt conflicted.

"You told me before that you like magic."

"Yeah, I do."

"I hated magic because of what it took from me. The same could be said for you, though. If magic didn't exist, you probably wouldn't be cursed right now."

"Uh-huh."

"Do you still like magic?"

"Yup, I love it. I'm almost grateful for it."

"What do you mean?"

I smiled and nodded.

"Remember when you asked me why I study magic? Well, I thought about my answer to that."

"Okay."

"To me, magic is what brings people together."

"It brings people together?"

"There are a ton of people I know only because of my magic. Including people I've saved, in a way. Sure, maybe the tears of joy were what sent me on this journey, but that's not all. I love helping people with my magic."

"If I remove magic from this world, it could save you, Spberry. Are you still against me doing that?"

"Yeah. I mean, I don't want to die, of course. But could you imagine how boring the world would be without magic? The same goes for you, I'm sure. We've both lived our lives for magic. I don't want to lose mine, and I don't want you to lose yours, either."

"Spberry..."

"There are people out there who are saved by magic and people who can only remain connected through it. It's the reason I met you and the reason we can help Wuf and Marie."

I never really thought about why I started magic; I kind of just went with the flow. But ever since I was told I only had one year to live, things changed. This was because there were things only I could do in this world, things magic allowed me to do.

I had the ability to help people in meaningful ways with my magic, and many people knew me because of this. Helping people with my magic gave my life meaning.

"What drives me is the people I love, and magic is my greatest ally when it comes to making their lives better."

"That's wrong!"

Sophie shook her head furiously like a child throwing a tantrum. Her face was scrunched up with anger, an expression I'd never seen her make before. It was like she'd been holding these emotions in the entire time, and they came exploding out of her. Perhaps her past was reminding her of what she lost.

"Magic is not an ally. It's trying to steal from me again. First my family, then my place, and now my friend..."

Sophie's legs buckled under her, and she fell to the ground, but I caught her. It felt like I captured much more than just her slender frame.

"I'm glad you consider me a friend."

"A friend, an assistant, a servant, a slave, a dog. It doesn't matter what you are—I don't want you to go."

"I think *friend* is a good word."

Sophie was ruthless even when she was sad. But her words made me happy, and she felt precious to me. I started patting her on the head and saying, "There, there. Everything will be all right. I won't die. I want to go to the Celebration of Worlds with you next year, too."

"I doubt I'll have space in my schedule to come again next year."

"Is that what you're worried about?" Sophie had her idiosyncrasies, but that's what I liked about her. "Let me make you a promise. That I'll live, no matter what."

"Really...?"

"Really. It's a promise. I can't let myself die yet."

It was another reason to live. The last thing I wanted to do before I died was break a promise.

I looked up to the sky as the twilight gave way to a starry night.

○

It was parade day.

The sun went down, and as soon as the beautiful full moon took its seat high in the night sky, Sophie stepped in front of the portal.

The outfit she wore for parades resembled military attire. I'd seen it online before, but when she wore it, she was like a completely different person—the Witch of Blessings, Sophie. The outfit made her more proper.

The portal would close at the end of the parade. The closure of the portal brought an end to what felt like a long dream.

A large crowd surrounded Sophie, granting her the necessary space as they watched in anticipation. I was among them, a spectator just as captivated.

Everyone was there, people from other worlds and our own. With all eyes fixed on Sophie, she lifted her hand and, in a manner akin to a fairy, began to spin, her movements resembling a dance. Orbs of light then started to gather around her. These were light Spirits, and I wasn't the only one who could see them. I could hear gasps of awe, the crowd utterly bewitched by the illusionary spectacle.

Spirits were normally invisible to the untrained eye, but Sophie made them visible to all. Borrowing power from the Spirits was a way to enhance and refine magic that created large-scale phenomena. This wasn't easy to do, though, and required immense amounts of magic. It was my first time even seeing Spirits in this way.

The light Spirits were poised to assist Sophie in orchestrating the parade. Once gathered, and as the crowd's anticipation reached its peak, they soared upward into the sky. Trails of light painted the sky with magnificent illusionary images. They spread in every direction, then the stream transformed, evaporating into tiny light particles that gently descended, morphing once again, this time into fluttering butterflies.

Butterflies of every color fluttered throughout the sky, filling it with bright and beautiful colors. This wasn't the end of the show, though. The town square where we stood was suddenly illuminated by the full moon. I quickly noticed that the light came from the ground where we stood; it was glowing faintly. It seemed like Sophie was using magic to capture the moon's light and shine it back from the ground.

It was almost like we were standing on top of the moon's reflection in a shallow pond.

"Ooooh," the crowd said collectively, and Sophie snapped her fingers, triggering a light to shine over the dimly lit city of Lapis. I now understood why we'd asked Mayor Carter to have lights turned off throughout the city. The magical light was some of the prettiest I'd ever seen.

Sophie continued the show with a display of magical fire spreading from her feet and radiating out toward the crowd. The illusionary flames weren't hot to touch, and they spread through the crowd only to disappear like a wave.

So much was happening all at once, both above and below the crowd, that it was almost hard to take it all in. The sheer level of skill behind the magic was astounding, lending an almost dreamlike quality to the entire experience.

Sophie captured the entire crowd with her magic. We all watched as the whole town was painted by a single witch. The crowd's awe could be heard throughout the chain of impossibly grand magic spells.

Sophie was such a talented mage that it was difficult to tell when she was even casting her spells. This was the power of a Sage. I found myself enthralled by the fluid motions she used to work her magic. Luckily, I was able to snap out of my stupor by lightly smacking my cheeks, because my part was coming up next.

I emerged from the crowd and stood next to Sophie, where I whistled. Carbuncle emerged from a different spot in the crowd, joining us at my feet. I touched my thumb gently to his forehead and quietly chanted a twelve-verse incantation.

The moment I finished, Carbuncle grew to an enormous size, turning into the largest creature anyone at the parade had ever seen.

I hopped onto his back and called out, "Come on out, everyone!"

My call was met with the appearance of hundreds upon hundreds of tiny woodland creatures from every nook and cranny in the city—they were my teacher's familiars. My little friends lined up in a perfect formation in front of me. It was time for the parade to begin.

"Onward, Carbuncle. Let's make rounds through the town."

"Squeak."

With me on his back, Carbuncle began to slowly march down the main road, followed by our woodland friends. The cute spectacle elicited a collective "Awww" from the crowd, and I knew the show was a hit.

As we progressed through the city, tiny magical spells I'd prepared beforehand went off. This included the falling of colorful snow in some places and individual bricks on the sides of buildings lighting up sporadically. The more the parade went on, the more Lapis was painted with illusions.

Much like Sophie's magic, Carbuncle's beautiful fur absorbed the moonlight, allowing him to shed a soft green light and making him into a spectacle himself.

As we moved forward, I could tell Sophie was still working her magic over the town square, as not a second went by when the sky wasn't displaying some sort of magical effect.

After visiting each corner of town, my parade of animals and magical effects worked its way back toward the town square, where we would hold our finale. The entire town of Lapis was filled to the brim with colorful magic at this point.

Everything progressed perfectly, and I eventually spotted a familiar face from atop Carbuncle's back. That face was heading to a spot where I'd promised I'd be.

"I'll leave the rest to you, partner."

"S-squeak?"

I'd be leaving Carbuncle in the lurch, but I knew he had this. All he needed to do was keep walking with the rest of the familiars, and the parade was good to go.

I had something else I needed to take care of.

I hopped off of giant Carbuncle and ran up to the person in question.

"Wuf, you came."

Wuf noticed me and removed his hood while he said, "Hey there, young witch." Maybe it was due to the full moon, but something about him seemed tougher than the first time we'd met.

"I was just heading to our meeting place, because I didn't want to break our promise. But is it really all right for you to be here right now? Don't you have a parade to run?"

"It'll be fiiine. This won't take long. I just have something to tell you."

"Oh?"

"A message from Marie. She's waiting for you at the place where you two watched the fireworks."

Wuf's eyes almost looked startled when he heard me say this.

"But I…"

"She said she doesn't care if you're a wolfman or whatever. She just wanted to watch fireworks with you again this year."

"But I thought there were no fireworks this year?"

I shook my head as he said this.

"Oh, there'll be fireworks all right."

"Are you sure…?"

"I promise."

Wuf looked up at the sky. "Okay, then. Seeing those fireworks up high in the sky used to give me hope and courage. Just looking at them alone gives me this kind of vigor to live. Even though I've been through a lot, they always bring me back, which is why I come here every year."

"Oh yeah?"

"Back when the townsfolk mistook me for an animal, I was spending the day with a little girl. I never forgot the fireworks we saw together. You know, Marie kind of reminded me of that little girl. It was the reason I noticed she wasn't feeling well the day I met her. This town's fireworks show is something special. It brought me and Marie together. But I didn't have courage that night. I was afraid of her seeing what I really am, so I ran away…"

"Do you think you'll have the courage to show her tonight?"

"I don't know. I was hoping there would be fireworks. I was hoping they could help give me the strength to accept my own feelings."

"I think you'll find that strength you need."

As I said this, I looked down at my wristwatch and noticed it was time to go.

"Wuf, I only ask that you make this a night that neither of you will regret. And if possible, I'd like for you two to watch the end of the parade together. I think you'll enjoy the fireworks you see tonight more than ever before."

"Young witch…"

"I have to go now. Just promise me this. You'll make a choice you'll never regret."

"Okay."

Wuf nodded, and I smiled back at him.
Then off I went, to finish the parade.

○

I needed to get back to the town square, but the closer I got, the thicker the crowd became, until I couldn't progress further. It seemed that after Carbuncle's procession, the onlookers all headed toward the town square to see the finale.

I was at a bit of a loss, when I noticed the highest point in Lapis—its clock tower.

"That's where I need to go…"

The clock tower marked the town's square. Going there would bring me where I needed to go, but the problem was, how was I gonna get there? At this rate, I was going to miss the finale. I could tell Sophie's magic was in its final phase.

This was when I noticed, however, that Sophie's magic wasn't all that was in the sky that night. I squinted, and lo and behold, there was White-Owl. He was flying inside the magic so as not to block the view, that wise little rascal.

"Hey! White-Owl! Over here!"

I waved my hand frantically at him, but he didn't notice at all.

"Okay, how about this?!"

I climbed up a nearby stone wall and whistled as loudly as I could, then noticed him veering toward me.

By the time he reached me, I'd already chanted a twelve-verse spell. Carefully timing my jump, I leaped from the stone wall, which made passersby gasp, but they had nothing to fear, for in the next instant, I was scooped up by a giant owl. They watched as I rode him high into the sky, and the gasps quickly turned to cheers and applause.

"How was that? Pretty cool, eh?"

White-Owl hooted apathetically in response to my question. Evidently, this wasn't enough for him, the cheeky owl.

"Let's get a move on! First, we'll go get Sophie!"

I pointed in the direction I wanted to go, and White-Owl cleared the distance to Sophie in a matter of seconds.

Sophie looked gobsmacked by the sudden appearance of a giant owl. White-Owl swooped down and picked her up, then brought her straight up into the air, and she let out a gruff "Oof!" that I wouldn't tease her for. The audience watched, *ooh*ing at the spectacle—it felt great to hear.

"How do you like them apples, Sophie? Can I put on a show, or can I put on a show?"

Sophie looked up at me with the enthusiasm of a dead fish.

"Spberry… Remind me to end your life later…"

Apparently, she didn't like being picked up against her will by a giant bird.

White-Owl brought us both to the clock tower. It was the best spot in town to see all of Lapis.

"There's a railing, but you can easily slip right through one of these gaps, so be careful not to fall."

"I will."

The crowd watched us from far below. The open space where Sophie once stood had already filled up as well. Everyone was ready for the grand finale.

"It's pretty up here," Sophie murmured softly as she looked up at the moon in the sky, and I could see her face clearly in its light.

"People aren't usually allowed to come up here save for the maintenance man who takes care of the clock. I guess it's another bonus to being a witch, eh?"

"There's lots of people out there tonight."

"They came to see us. I bet just as many...no, more people come to see the parades you always conduct."

Sophie looked out at the crowd with a distant gaze.

"When I hold these parades, it always reminds me of how happy it makes people. It's funny, but seeing the crowd like this makes me happy, too. It's times like these when I find myself appreciating the magic I'm supposed to hate so much."

"Do you really hate magic as much as you say you do, Sophie?"

"What makes you say that?"

"If you really hated it, you wouldn't have put so much effort into mastering it," I said, then hopped onto White-Owl's back, leaving her on the clock tower. "I, for one, love your magic, Sophie. You should really be more confident in yourself."

"You're one to talk."

Sophie's shoulders slumped; she seemed almost stunned by my remark. I always enjoyed our banter.

"All right, I'll leave you to do your thing."

I gave White-Owl a signal, and he flapped his wings, ascending into the sky.

The parade was about to get physical. I constructed white orbs of magic, which I released into the sky, each orb harboring multicolored magic. I dropped a big batch of them, and from atop the clock tower, Sophie let loose a magical arrow that struck true.

And then the real magic happened—a flower of light blossomed in the festive night sky. It let fly multiple beams of bright, beautiful light that flashed across the heavens. The vivid burst of light triggered the surrounding orbs I'd dropped, setting off a chain reaction that quickly filled the air.

I was almost captivated by the incredible result of my own show, but I didn't have time to get distracted—I needed to get the next batch ready. Without a second to spare, I made more orbs, sent Sophie our signal, she fired her arrow, and the sky lit up once more.

We did this without rest, keeping the sky illuminated with brilliant blooms. White-Owl flew through the air, and I made magical orbs as quickly as I could.

One hundred, two hundred…at some point, I lost count. I could feel myself getting a sort of runner's high from how lively it was. It was certainly far more than I'd ever made during practice, but for some reason, I didn't feel tired at all, and I could also feel that I was pushing myself further than I'd ever gone.

The end, however, always comes abruptly.

I didn't know how many fireworks we sent up, but out of nowhere, my consciousness began to falter. My vision blurred, and I was seeing double. I had used too much magic.

It all happened much quicker than I ever could've imagined. I didn't have time to try and fight it or even push through it. I fell to one knee, which sank deep into White-Owl's feathers.

Sophie has been using magic all night and still has a spring in her step, but I can barely hold on. I just hope Wuf and Marie saw our fireworks…

Just when I felt my vision going black and I was about to pass out, I could feel someone prop me up.

It was my teacher.

"I must admit, you did well, Meg."

"Teacher? Why are you here…?"

"I wouldn't be able to call myself a teacher if I wasn't at least aware of my pupil's condition."

So you saw this coming. Nothing ever gets by you, huh?

"Are you going to take over…?

"Of course not. Tonight is your night."

After my teacher said this, she held up her hand as if to give a signal, and I noticed Sophie answer with a nod. Despite being barely conscious, I could tell there was a strange magical reaction surging throughout Sophie's entire body.

"She'll take care of the rest for you."

I felt like Sophie heard my teacher say this.

Because then it happened.

The magic Sophie harbored burst out of her, filling the sky in its entirety all at once. And it just kept coming—each burst bigger and louder than before.

"Whoa..."

"You should watch this, Meg. This is Sophie's true power. You were able to release five thousand of your own fireworks. Sophie will take care of the remaining twenty-five thousand."

"Ha-ha... You Seven Sages don't disappoint..."

The field of blossoming fireworks reminded me of the shows from past years.

"It's strange, Teacher... I was able to create way more fireworks...than when we...practiced. I had way...more power... than I normally do..."

Something about what I said made my teacher pleased, because she smiled before speaking.

"Magic is strongest when it carries the feelings from your heart," she said before taking her eyes off me and looking down. "See for yourself." She propped me up to look down, and in an instant, I knew exactly what she meant.

There stood Wuf and Marie, watching the fireworks together—watching us. Wuf had his hood down, which told me he was able to come out of his shell and show his true self to Marie.

And Marie accepted him for it.

"I'm glad they could meet up... You know, Teacher...magic exists to make people happy, doesn't it?"

"Of course. That's why we witches are here."

As she said this, I realized something else.

Sophie, who usually wore a stony expression, was looking our way with a big smile on her face.

And I reciprocated her infectious smile by smiling back.

And this was how the Celebration of Worlds came to an end.

○

"The town and I owe you so much!"

Mayor Carter came to visit the manor the day after the festival, and as soon as the door opened, he bowed his head and said, "This has been one of Lapis's most successful festivals ever, and it was all thanks to you, Sophie! With all the extra media coverage, I'm willing to bet we'll have a big festival next year, too!"

"That's nice."

"I agree. I was worried about how things would turn out this year when I was injured, but I'm really glad you pulled through for us."

"Lady Faust is right…"

Mayor Carter said this before turning his gaze to me.

"So, uh, what exactly is wrong with Meg?"

While the three chatted, I was lying on the living room sofa. My body was all jiggly and wobbly like it was made of slime, and I was completely limp. I had barely any life in me.

My teacher and Sophie calmly looked over at me as they sipped their tea.

"That is what happens when a witch uses more magic than she can handle. She made the same mistake during the portal ceremony, too. Sometimes, it's hard to believe she's my pupil."

"Spberry is a bit slow. That's why she repeats the same mistakes."

"Waaah! I can't mooove!"

"Ah-ha-ha… It looks like she's having a bit of trouble."

When this happened during the portal ceremony, I got away with a nosebleed and some dizziness, but this time was completely different. Evidently, depending on what magic you used, the symptoms of overexerting yourself changed. Talk about a pain.

While I lay on the sofa lifeless and limp, Sophie came over and started poking my forehead.

"Stop that..."

"This is fun," she said before pinching and stretching my cheeks.

"Staaahp!"

"There's nothing more entertaining than teasing someone who can't fight back."

"Stop, please! Miss! Waaah! Teacher, help me!"

"Hopefully this will be a lesson in mana management."

My teacher left me with this and turned her attention back to the mayor.

"So, Mayor. May I ask what brings you here today?"

"Huh? Oh, well, I just wanted to thank you personally for yesterday..."

"I know it's not only that. They call me the Eternal Witch for a reason, you know."

"Ah... All right, all right. I've brought some guests with me who wish to see you."

Guests? The sudden conversation caught both my and Sophie's attention.

Mayor Carter then called over to the front door, "You may come in now."

It was quiet for a moment, but then two figures appeared at the front door.

"Wuf... What are you doing here...?"

I spoke without thinking, but his presence caught me completely off guard. After all, the portal was already closed, and people not of this world should've returned to their own homes by now.

"Hello…young witch."

"We're sorry for barging in like this."

I was completely confused, but the mayor came forward, taking out a piece of paper from his jacket pocket. It wasn't just any paper, but one made of animal hide…parchment made of sheep, to be specific.

"I'd like to inform you that these two submitted an application to our Special Affairs Division…"

"So it's a *contract*? That's rare, in this day in age."

A contract.

Sophie and I both heard my teacher say it, and we began to speculate.

At the end of the Celebration of Worlds, anyone who wasn't of this world was sent back to their own. If they didn't return via the portal, their body would slowly disappear over the next few days, and they would cease to exist.

People not of this world weren't supposed to exist here—they were irregular. This was why when the portal that tethered them here disappeared, the laws of this world…would soon begin to reject their existence.

A person whose existence wasn't accepted by the world was fated to disappear. It happened slowly, their presence growing unclear, until they simply ceased to be there at all. The person would live on, though, as a ghostly form of themself. There wouldn't be a way for them to interact with anything tangible, and they would eventually starve to death or, if that wouldn't kill them, wander the world as a ghost for eternity.

There was no way to interact with a world that was not your own. This was why the visitors only came once a year for the Celebration of Worlds and would return home when it finished.

There were, however, a select few who wished to stay in this world, and for them, there was the contract. These interlopers needed to wear shackles that monitored them so they didn't do anything wrong in this world. Those shackles, however, also allowed for this world's laws to recognize their existence and gave them the power to remain here.

"I've learned that these two fell in love during this year's festival and have applied to live together in our world. I thought I would bring them here to introduce you."

Well, look at that. Those two wanna live here, eh?

My teacher, as if she could read my mind, turned to me.

"I trust you have something to do with this, Meg."

"Oh, yeah…"

Hearing this, the mayor responded, "Well, that should make this easy, then. If Miss Raspberry is involved with their relationship, then there's no need for me to explain it."

"Whatever the case may be, it does not change what we shall do. The contract is simple, so long as both parties agree to it," my teacher said, Wuf and Marie watching quietly as she stood before them. "However, a man and woman brought together by fleeting emotions are liable to come back, begging me to end their contract… I've seen it before. I cannot bind you two so flippantly. Whatever happens, you will be in this world for a minimum of one year. This is a serious commitment, and it is one I trust you are both willing to make?"

My teacher said this as if to prod the couple's feelings. Her gaze was stern—she would see through any lie or deception. If either of them spoke without thinking, my teacher would know.

"Faust."

It was Sophie who broke the mounting tension.

"These two will be fine. You have my word."

"It's awfully rare for you to say such a thing."

With Sophie's unexpected remark, the tension in my teacher's expression eased.

"But if Sophie insists, then I have no reason to doubt her judgment."

"Well then, Lady Faust. I take it this means…"

My teacher nodded at the mayor's words.

"Yes. I will bind them via the contract."

The smiles on both Marie's and Wuf's faces looked genuinely happy when they heard this. They looked at each other and exchanged those smiles. My teacher observed them and then took out a pair of reading glasses before scanning the parchment.

"Now, who will be their witness?"

"T-Teacher… If you would allow me…"

I barely managed to say this but was rejected by my teacher. "Don't be foolish. Look at yourself; you're a wobbly blob. To form the contract requires a certain amount of mana, I'll have you know. In your current state, you would probably flub it up."

"Nooo…"

"It's fine. I'll do it." Sophie gently took the parchment out of my teacher's hands. "I want you to let me do it."

"Oh? That's fine by me, but are you sure?"

"I am."

"Well then, go ahead."

I watched with awe as Sophie filled out the parchment, then used a knife to cut her finger and stamped the page with her own blood.

"I have one request."

Sophie turned to Wuf and Marie with a stern look on her face.

"I want you to promise me you'll both be happy."

"Yes… We can promise that."

Hearing this, Sophie gave them a big smile, then held her hand over the parchment and chanted her spell.

"Upon my name I ask thee to act, bind these two souls by contract."

When she said this, a ring that fit perfectly appeared on the ring fingers of both Wuf's and Marie's hands.

"What's this…?" asked Marie in confusion.

Sophie nodded to her.

"It is proof of the contract. It is proof that you swore to the world that you would be together, and it has accepted your promise."

"Proof…"

"You need to take care of your rings. So long as you keep them on, you can always be together."

The couple looked at each other's rings. Even though they'd thought they would never see each other again, the world had accepted that they could live together.

For Wuf and Marie, this must've felt like a lifelong dream coming true.

The large tears that ran down each of their faces spoke more to this than anything.

"Finally… We can be together."

"I'll never let you go. Never."

The two shared the heartfelt, tearful moment together.

And they shared two tears with me, which fell into my bottle.

○

"I'll be off, then."

Soon after Wuf, Marie, and the mayor left, Sophie decided to leave for London. She had another parade there waiting for her.

My body had finally recovered, and I accompanied my teacher to the door where we saw her off.

"You really helped out this time. Thank you."

"Come by anytime you want to hang out. I'll make sure to have some delicious treats on hand."

"I look forward to it."

Just as she was about to go, something occurred to me, and I called out to her, "Sophie. There's something I want to ask you before you go."

"What?"

"Why did you decide to be Wuf and Marie's witness?"

My question seemed to catch her by surprise, as she looked back at me.

"What do you mean?"

"You just don't seem like the type to get involved with that kind of thing."

"Well… It's your fault, really."

"My fault?"

"I figured if I took a page from your magic-loving book, maybe I could learn to love it, too. That's why I used my magic to help them."

The expression on Sophie's face as she said this made her seem like a different person from when I met her. She was trying to change, taking baby steps to face her past.

"So how'd it feel? Do you like magic now?"

"Nope. Actually, it was kind of a pain. I still hate magic, but…" She smiled. "I don't think I want to remove it from the world anymore." Sophie's eyes were locked with mine. "Just as you said magic was a way for you to connect with people, I've connected to my friend with magic."

"Sophie…"

"Spberry. I want you to promise me one thing. You're not allowed to die until I say it's okay. If you die before that, I'll kill you. Even if I have to chase you into the afterlife."

"That makes no sense…"

You know, Inori said something similar. Maybe all Sages think alike?

Well, that aside.
"That's what I intend to do anyway."

We watched Sophie go until we could no longer see her, then my teacher remarked, "And there she goes. Perhaps what Sophie needed most was not an adult who understood her, or a teacher, but a friend her own age."
"Is that why you asked for her to be your replacement?"
"That, my child, shall remain a mystery."
My teacher had a way of shrugging off the big questions.
Would it hurt to entertain your apprentice once in a while?
I was giving her a mean stare from behind when she changed the topic once more. "About that wolfman. It seems he's pursuing a career in fireworks."
"He's going to be a fireworks maker?"
"Yes, he told me it was what he did in his own world, too. It seems that with our town's fireworks maker gone, he wants to take up the mantle."
"Wait, do you think…?"
"That he became a fireworks maker because of the fireworks here? That's precisely the reason."
I removed the bottle from my belt. There were two more tears in my collection. They were Wuf's and Marie's.
"It's funny how things come full circle, isn't it?"
"Oh, is that all you collected during the celebration?"
"Huh?"
"You were talking as if you were going to acquire all one thousand during the festivities."
"Oh crap! Darn it! This is nothing!"
I'd completely forgotten about my scheme to use Sophie to collect one thousand tears during the festival. I slumped over in dismay but soon felt a sympathetic tap on my shoulder.

"Thanks to you, the town will have fireworks again next year. I must admit, you did quite well."

With a smile, she continued. "Not bad. Not bad at all."

With the festival over, everything was back to normal in the town of Lapis—save for a few small details.

A young girl who hated magic had begun to accept it.

Two souls long separated managed to reunite and were now determined to live together.

And I had a new, precious friend.

I closed my eyes tightly, and I could see a clear new vision. It was of next year's festival, and I was there.

I went back to my everyday life with an even stronger desire to live on.

Chapter 7: An Evening Sky Without Magic

The Eternal Witch, Lady Faust, reigned at the pinnacle of magic as one of the Seven Sages, but for the past few days, an eerie cackle had echoed throughout her manor.

"Eh-heh… Hee-hee-hee… Ha-ha…"

This laugh was sinister, emanating from the darkest shadows, and with each passing day, it grew louder. It was akin to the darkness of the dead of night.

"Ooo-hee-hee-hee, ha-ha!!"

"Argh! Will you stop doing that, Meg?!"

I was grinning to myself in my room when my teacher burst in. She was absolutely livid.

"What's the matter? Why would you barge in on me all mad during my alone time?"

"Because you're laughing all night like a complete lunatic!"

"You're upset with my laugh…? What's wrong with the beautiful laugh of a young seventeen-year-old maiden such as myself?"

"You sound like a forty-year-old man chortling to yourself in here. And it's not just me; the familiars have had enough of your antics as well."

"The animals?"

My teacher then produced a letter and handed it to me. I opened it and found a note written in tiny, scribbled handwriting that said, *Please do something about Meg's annoying laugh.*

"Whoa, this is actually impressive. I didn't know the familiars could write… Right, White-Owl?"

White-Owl flinched when I said this.

"There aren't many of them who can read, after all. But I remember you teaching yourself how to read. By the way, Teacher. Did you know they put birds on skewers and roast them in the East? They eat the wings, the skin, and even the rump."

The more I said with my monotone voice, the more White-Owl began to tremble. I half expected him to start having a little seizure, when my teacher quietly stepped in. "Enough. There is no reason to take this out on your familiar. And he's right. Your laughing is very disturbing."

"That's just how I laugh, though…"

My teacher then shifted her eyes to my tear bottle on my desk.

"Well, would you look at that? Your collection is growing. Is this what has you laughing so often?"

"Pretty much, yeah."

There were thirty tear shards inside my bottle. My teacher picked it up and gave it a gentle shake.

"Twenty-two of these appear to be tears of joy, and eight from other emotions, it looks like."

"Do those eight end up being useless to me?"

"We'll have to see… All the tears you've collected thus far are pure, so there may be a way to substitute them in."

"Oh, that's a relief. It's impossible enough to get a thousand tears when you have no idea what kind of tears you're gonna get."

"Shards of emotion are just that powerful."

"You know, I've been wondering what these shards of emotion are in the first place. Inori had no idea, and I can't find a book that has much about them, either. I don't really know where else to look."

There was nothing on the tears needing to be of joy and what the concept of purity meant. I didn't know what my teacher was looking at when she inspected my tears.

The only thing I knew was that shards of emotion were no longer used in modern magic, which was why they were so mysterious.

When I asked about them, my teacher's expression appeared somewhat lonely.

"Mages no longer know about shards of emotion. It's been long forgotten in the pages of time—what mages should aim for…and what's important."

"What do you mean by that?"

"That, my child, you will have to figure out on your own. For now, you should focus on collecting as many tears as you can."

As my teacher said this, she examined the bottle with an upset look on her face. She then shook the bottle, as if inspecting it for something in particular.

"How did you get these tears anyway?"

"Huh? You know, helping people, hearing them out… Lots of things. It was tough collecting just those thirty alone, you know."

"I must say, you've been able to gather quite a few in a short time."

"Yeah, you get used to it after a while." I nodded smugly. "I've got a nose for this sort of thing now. Such as noticing a mum with a bratty kid, or an elderly woman having trouble walking. I try to find people who look like they will need help soon. I also got one by simply being nice to a salesman who was feeling stressed out from work. It's getting pretty easy."

"You sure seem confident in yourself."

"What can I say? This is what *getting good* looks like. I mean, I even helped Sophie pull off one of the biggest jobs ever."

Ever since the Celebration of Worlds and its parade, I'd

improved my magic control. Although I overexerted myself during the portal ceremony and parade, through practice, I was beginning to better manage my mana.

With my knowledge of magic gradually growing, using different magic spells was no longer so imposing an endeavor. This was what gave me confidence.

"Meg, you aren't allowed to use magic until I say so."

"Huh?"

I was left dumbfounded by my teacher's sudden decree, but she seemed unfazed by my reaction. I weakly opened my mouth to question her.

"Wh-why, though?"

My voice was shaking while I said this.

"Because at this rate, it will ruin you."

"Why's that...?"

"Place your hand on your heart and think. You need to find this answer for yourself. Me simply telling you holds no significance."

With that, my teacher left the room—leaving me alone.

"What the heck?" No one was there to answer. "I don't... What?"

○

"What am I supposed to do now?"

With a *thump*, I placed my forehead on the table where I sat. My companion Carbuncle gave me a cute "*Squeak*" of encouragement before jumping onto the back of my head. My friend Fine sat at the other side of the table with a cup of black tea and a surprised look on her face.

I was at her house, ranting about my troubles.

"Here I thought she was impressed with the number of tears I'd collected, then she hits me with a rule that I can't use magic anymore. I don't know what to think! I swear, I'm gonna smack that old woman when I get home."

"Let's be civil… Surely she's doing this for you, right? I doubt Lady Faust is the type to be strict just to take you down a notch."

"Well, yeah… That's true."

Fine was right; everything my teacher did had meaning. Whenever she had me do something, there was also a rhyme and reason to it.

Like it would teach me a lesson or help me realize something.

That was why this time, I just needed to figure out what that something was.

I knew the importance of being able to think on my own—it was something my teacher had taught me.

"Maybe she doesn't want you using your magic for evil."

"There's no way. She'd kill me if I did that anyway. I've been using magic for years."

"Maybe someone in town filed a complaint about you?"

"I don't think so. I mean, all I'm doing is making people cry tears of joy. If someone files a complaint for that, I'm countersuing."

"Hmm, this is hard…"

Fine breathed a small sigh before cocking her head at a new thought.

"How hard is it to get someone to cry tears of joy anyway?"

"It was tough until I figured out the trick to it. Little girls and overworked businessmen are pretty easy to get to cry if you know how to work 'em."

"You sound more like a con artist than a tear artist."

Fine, shocked by my words, smiled awkwardly as she drank her tea before murmuring, "It's a shame, though. To hear you talking about people's tears like that. I never pegged you as the type to talk about people like this."

"Why's that?"

"Don't you think tears of joy are something a person only sheds when they are at their happiest? I liked it better when you treated each and every tear with more significance."

Each and every tear is significant.

This struck a chord.

"I mean, I don't think I treat these tears any different."

"That's good, if you say so."

In a way, she was right. With every tear I collected, I was growing more apathetic. The feeling when I got my first tear compared to the more recent ones was not quite the same. But that didn't mean I considered the newer ones any less important. The only reason there was a problem at all was because the animals told on me when I was gazing at my bottle of tears every night with glee.

At the same time, I recognized that maybe my glee wasn't for the tears themselves but how validated I felt as I acquired more and more. Maybe I was happier with the sheer number of tears I was pulling in than anything else…

"You need to hold each and every tear dear to yourself."

Fine followed with this soft statement, as if she could see right through my introspection.

"I need one thousand in a year, though? It's a massive challenge even without my life being on the line. Don'cha think it's kind of impossible to put that much focus on the tears themselves?"

"Yeah, you're probably right, but Lady Faust said you were going to ruin yourself at this rate, right? Maybe the value of your tears comes from the value you place in them?"

"I think they're different. It's not like the tears I've collected have changed at all."

While I rejected her guess, I wasn't confident in myself as I said it.

Seeing this, Fine smiled gently.

"What're you smilin' about? Can't ya see I'm depressed here?"

"Sorry, it's just funny that despite how upset you are with Lady Faust's decision, you still obey her. You're a lot more diligent than you let on. It's a bit fun to watch."

"Listen 'ere, toots. Ya wanna watch something fun, go to a movie theater."

As I joked with Fine, she noticed the time on her watch and stood up, saying, "Oh no. I'm sorry, I just remembered I have an appointment after this."

"What's so important that you're gonna leave your best friend high and dry? It better not be a date with some guy."

"Oh, uh… Kinda?"

"Wait, seriously?"

"I'll tell you about it later."

I left Fine's house, though it was more like she kicked me out. With the sudden news taking a heavier toll on me than I predicted, I wandered aimlessly through town.

Fine has a boyfriend? I didn't know she was seeing anybody. I've never dated anyone before, either. My friend's becoming an adult…

"I don't know what I expected. Fine is a student, and I am some old lady's assistant…"

As I walked along with my shoulders slumped, my two familiars found their way to me.

"All I have is you two."

I squatted down to pet them, and they both closed their eyes in happiness.

"The last thing I want to become, though, is some crazy cat lady, or familiar lady in my case."

As soon as I said this, I watched as my two familiars quickly shifted to try and distance themselves. White-Owl managed to fly away, but Carbuncle wasn't so fortunate. I picked him up by the scruff of his neck and brought his face close to mine, but he did everything he could to keep our eyes from meeting.

"I'm in the mood for meat for dinner tonight."

I could feel through Carbuncle's scruff that a shudder ran down his spine.

○

As I meandered down the street with nowhere in mind to go, I left Lapis's residential area and entered downtown. Here, markets, restaurants, apparel stores, and other places to shop lined the streets. Even though it was the middle of a weekday, it was relatively busy, with a mix of housewives, elderly citizens, and businesspeople in suits.

"Hey, this was the spot where I got my last tear."

I thought back to a few days earlier, when I'd visited the town square.

The man was young and dressed in a suit. He was hired by his company soon after graduating from college but had to work late into the night every night because of how tough the work was. I came across him just after his first major negotiation—one he had painstakingly managed to organize—had unfortunately fallen through. He was sitting on a bench, a picture of dejection, seemingly unable to muster the strength to return to his company. Seeing him sitting in the cold, I handed him a cup of coffee, heard him out, and then made him some incense to try and cheer him up.

Reflecting back on it, something I said to him made him shed a tear of joy at some point during the exchange.

"No one's been kind to me in so long."

I'm pretty sure it was something like that.

"He said something like that, right?" I asked Carbuncle, and he shook his head. His attitude suggested it wasn't that he didn't remember but that he didn't know. He probably wasn't listening when the man and I spoke.

"Hmm, well, for him to cry, I must've said something really touching. Maybe for a guy new to his company, having a young seventeen-year-old girl hear him out when he was at his lowest was enough to cheer him up."

Carbuncle shook his head at this remark as well.

Well, what do you *know?*

Setting that aside, all I did was hear the man out. Nothing more, nothing less. I could hardly remember what he looked like, which made me feel sort of bad.

I needed to bring in more tears. I didn't have time to pay attention to things like details or faces. Building relationships with people took time and energy, two things I was running short on.

"There's a big difference between spending a bunch of time only to get one tear and banging 'em out one after another—a difference that could mean life or death for me. I don't have time to be concerned more with the journey than the reward, right?"

"Squeak?"

I'd already wasted too much of what little time I had. Despite a need to find a way to make up for lost time, my teacher wasn't going to let me use magic.

"Ugh… Maybe I *should* just use magic."

Only a few days had passed since the end of the Celebration of Worlds. The reason I was able to accumulate so many tears so quickly was partially due to luck but mainly thanks to my talent as a mage. I was beginning to think that maybe I could get the tears I needed without my teacher. At the same time, a part of me knew this wasn't the case.

"Hello there, Meg."

I snapped out of my deep thoughts and looked up to find an old man I'd never met before standing before me. Actually, he did seem kind of familiar… Who was he again?

"Oh, hello."

I returned his hello and continued walking. Not far from there, however, an old woman did the same and said, "Hello, Meg. Thank you for the other day." I didn't know who she was, either.

"Ah, ha-ha, don't mention it."

Once more, I hurried along to get away.

"Oh, if it isn't Meg."

"Hello, Miss Witch."

"Meg, thanks for the other day."

"Ah! Meg!"

"Meeeg, waaait!"

"It's always good to see you doing well, Meg."

What's going on? It feels like I'm running into somebody I barely know every other block.

It wasn't rare for people to greet me on my trips to the city, but it was starting to get weird today. This was already double the number of people who usually greeted me, an amount I'd never experienced before.

I had an idea what the reason could be, though: the parade Sophie and I held.

Sophie Hayter. One of the Seven Sages and a young genius who shook the world. With her captivating beauty and unfathomable magical prowess, the public loved her—and I'd had the chance to hold a parade here in Lapis with her.

The parade was enough for our town to be all over the news, so it made sense that people I didn't know now recognized me.

"I didn't realize everyone was so in the loop with the latest news. I guess people are more easily starstruck than I thought. Most of these people wouldn't talk to me had I not been a part of the parade."

"Squeak?"

This comment seemed to confuse Carbuncle, who cocked his head to the side. He looked like he wanted to say something.

What do you *know?*

We left the market area and continued down the street to where the train station was. This was the only railroad in Lapis, and it connected to the neighboring big cities. With the trains being easily subject to inclement weather, there were already plans to create a subway system, but it was going to take a long time before they finished. Certainly not in my lifetime.

My aimless meandering brought me there. Usually, I would be running errands, taking care of the plants, or studying magic around this time, but I didn't have any motivation.

This was when I caught sight of a woman pushing a stroller. She seemed young and was the type of person I usually profiled for my tear-jerking shenanigans as of late. I'd watch to see when she might need help, then swoop in when the chance presented itself.

While I thought this, our eyes met, and she appeared to smile at me.

Who's she smiling at? Me?

I was so caught off guard by this that I looked around for someone else. I didn't want to wave at her only for someone she knew to pop up from behind me—that'd be embarrassing.

It wasn't the case, though, because I was the only person there. She seemed to be smiling at me.

There's no way that smile's for me, though, right?

C'mon, Meg, we need to remember. I bet we know her.

We definitely do not. I have no memory of her.

Way to sound like a corrupt politician feigning ignorance in court.

Yeah right. We were never the sharpest tool in the shed.

Hey, don't be mean.

The Megs in my mind held an emergency meeting.

While the many iterations of me in my mind bickered among themselves, the woman approached me. When I took notice of this, the Megs from the meeting all screamed and started running around like chickens with their heads cut off.

"Miss Witch! I'm glad to see you again! Thank you so much for the other day."

The woman grabbed my hand and gave me a big smile.

"Yeah, nooo. It's fiiine, ha-ha-ha," I replied, trying to play it cool despite my confusion. What was she talking about? Maybe she was mistaking me for a different witch? The only two witches in town were my teacher and I…

"You really saved me."

"Mm-hmm, always glad to help when I can."

"Do you have a minute? I'd really like to thank you, maybe buy you a cup of tea."

"Ah, uh…"

I tried to say no but couldn't quite find the words. My muddled brain couldn't come up with a reason to reject her offer.

"I've actually been looking for you, so I'm glad I finally found you."

"Oh… Thanks."

○

The two of us entered a nice little café near the station. It was a bit awkward to be drinking tea with someone I didn't know.

"I'm so thankful you came when you did. I don't know what I would've done without you."

"I-is that right?"

It looked like I was going to have to go all in on this. I would talk to her and try to fish for details to help me remember who she was.

You got this, Meg Raspberry.

"That was a doozy… About your baby…"

"Ah yes. The little one can be such a ball of energy."

"But it's a good thing we found her."

"I'm sorry? Found her?"

"No, I mean you found me! I actually wanted to see you again, after all! Ah-ha-ha!"

"Yes, me too. I'm happy that Lapis has a witch like you, because were it not for you, my husband and I would've gotten into a big fight."

"Family first, eh?"

"I agree. So many couples nowadays break up over the tiniest of things, so I was really worried."

"Well, you know men. They have their little stints with women here and there…"

"Women?

"Not that your husband did!"

This is hell. Somebody, please save me.

A cold sweat began running down my back, when the woman suddenly took a familiar-looking pocket watch out of her pocket and set it on the table.

"Here it is, by the way. The watch you fixed. It still works."

This helped me remember who she was: the watch lady from the other day.

Her baby accidentally broke the watch, which was a gift from the woman's mother-in-law. It wasn't the baby who broke the watch, though, but simply that the Spirits within had disappeared.

She seemed distraught over it, so I approached her and replaced the watch's Spirits, allowing it to start working again.

When she saw the watch working again, she must've cried from the relief she felt.

"So it wasn't actually broken but just lost its Spirits. Do I have that right?"

"Yeah, Spirits can be finicky. Some Spirits just don't like watches, so I called for some that do and got an answer, I guess you could say..."

The more we spoke about it, the more I remembered.

That's right, this lady reminded me of Fine. I figured if I helped her fix her watch, she would maybe cry a tear of joy for me.

It was a simple thought process but exactly what happened.

It's not as if I was taking advantage of her or anything, but there was no pure desire to help this woman for the sake of helping her.

I'd just wanted tears, that's all. Tear farming had become a daily task for me, not even a mission. I figured I could simplify the process based on my past experiences. The more I reflected on it, the worse I felt about how shallow I'd been. It was like the guilt wrapped tightly around my heart.

While skills and experience were needed to help people, this only related to magic itself and had little to do with the inner workings of human emotion.

"You get used to it after a while. I figured out the trick to it."

Get used to what? What trick is there to figure out?

At some point, I'd lost touch with myself. I could feel my face getting hot as I realized this.

In the beginning, I felt so happy when I received pure emotion from somebody else. It was what let me know I was truly helping them.

When did it happen? When did I stop looking at the face of the person I was trying to help? When did I stop caring about *them*?

* * *

We left the café, and the woman headed for the train station. I learned that she wasn't even from this town and that she just so happened to be here to buy something on the day we met. Evidently, she'd come all the way back, just in search of me.

"Are you okay, Miss Witch? You don't look so well."

"Huh? Oh… Yeah, I'm fine."

The woman seemed worried about me. She leaned in to get a better look at my face, and it was the first time I really looked at hers.

She was a beautiful young woman with a mole next to one of her eyes. There was genuine kindness in her gaze; she gave off an air of purity. This should've been what I thought on the day we met, and realizing I was only taking this in now served to confuse me more.

She wasn't just pretty but stunningly beautiful. So much so that I was starting to stutter even though we were both girls. I was starting to get nervous simply being next to her—that's how pretty she was.

So I wasn't even looking at people's faces when I was on the prowl for tears? I must've filtered them out while I talked with them.

I was sure this woman wasn't the only person I'd done this to. I couldn't remember the faces of anyone I'd helped the past few days. The only thing I saw in people was personal gain. That was it.

Ever since the festival ended, I was blinded by pride in myself as a witch. I realized I'd been full of myself because of what I'd accomplished.

"Are you sure you're all right? You seem upset about something. I'll lend you an ear if you need someone to talk to."

"No, it's nothing really…uh…Miss."

"Rachael."

"Huh?"

"That's my name. We haven't exchanged them yet."

"Ah, I'm Meg. Meg Raspberry."

"Meg. Heh, it's funny to introduce ourselves now after all this time."

"You're right."

I didn't even introduce myself when we met. That's how oblivious I'd been.

"You are a witch who can open the hearts of others."

I remembered what my teacher had said to me a while back. I wasn't sure if this was the case anymore.

"Rachael. What do you do when you think you've done something wrong?" I asked her without really thinking about it.

Rachael seemed caught off guard by my question.

"Something wrong?"

"How should I put it? Like when someone everyone calls nice is actually doing things for other people for their own gain without even realizing it themselves, but then they suddenly realize who they really are."

This time, she seemed utterly confused, which made sense. This wasn't something that happened every day.

"Sorry, I didn't mean to ask you such a strange question. You can just forget about it."

Rachael shook her head, though, and began to respond.

"If that person thinks what they did was wrong, then they should probably accept that they were wrong and start over again."

"Start over..."

"Everyone makes mistakes. I think what's important is how you change after you do."

"Do you think I can change?"

"I'm sure of it, if you really want to."

Rachael then smiled, and it was like the smile of a goddess.

○

I escorted Rachael to the train turnstile before continuing my slow walk through town. I was feeling gloomy, despite her having cheered me up a bit. I didn't really know what to make of it. I was never one to let myself get upset like this. Worrying too much about things wasn't in my nature. I just wanted to think about something else, but it felt like there was a weight on my heart.

My aimless wandering brought me to a staircase that led to one of the highest points in town. This spot was far from the center of town, where my walk began, and it was somewhere I rarely visited.

At the bottom of the stairs was an old woman carrying a big paper bag. She was sitting down, and it was clear that she needed a helping hand. At the same time, I knew helping her probably wouldn't earn me a tear. No one in their right mind would cry over some groceries.

"Hello there, Granny. Do you need a hand?"

I asked her if she needed help anyway. Maybe I wouldn't have if I were the same as I'd been earlier. I probably would've left her to her own devices in search of more tears.

But not anymore—I needed to change, and this would be my first step. I wanted to start over again.

It didn't matter if the woman wasn't going to cry after I helped her. There was a version of me who asked if she needed help and one who didn't, and I wanted to be the one who did.

I wanted to be proud of who I was.

* * *

"Mrgh! This is so heavy!"

It was a long set of stairs, and I had the old woman on my back while I carried her bag in my hands. Evidently, this old woman lived on top of the highest hill in town.

"Are you all right? You don't need to carry me. Want me to get off?"

"There's no need! A girl also keeps her word!"

As I spoke, my breath came out in heavy pants, visible in the cold air. Despite the chilly temperature, sweat trickled down my forehead. My breath formed white clouds in the frigid air, and I noticed a bit of snot running from my nose.

Why am I, a witch, partaking in such manual labor? Situations like this are what magic is for! I thought to myself in exhaustion.

I could make the groceries weigh nothing using antigravity magic or use a muscle-enhancement spell to make these stairs a cakewalk...though the soreness I'd experience the next day would be a killer.

I think I've learned my lesson today. I've reflected on what I've done wrong and am trying to better myself for it.

So maybe I should just do it—use magic.

I could hear the devil whispering temptation in the back of my mind. I shook my head, freeing it from the devil's grip, and focused on the task at hand.

I was trying to restart. Making this trip up this steep hill was like a ceremony for me to get back up while I was down.

"Agh, I'm knackered."

After finally making it to the top and setting both the groceries and the grandmother down, I limply slumped onto the ground like a pile of sludge. I rolled over, looking up at the sky to see the first few stars of the night faintly make their appearance as the day quickly turned into night. With nothing but the setting sun to warm me, the wind was cold but somehow comfy at the same time.

"You must be, after that."

The old woman hobbled over, peering down at me on the ground.

"I do appreciate it. Those stairs aren't usually a problem for me, but I hurt my back recently. I should probably start thinking about my age."

"You think you can make the rest of the trip alone?"

"Yes. I really do appreciate what you've done for me."

With a smile, the old woman took a seat on one of the steps.

"You're Meg, Lady Faust's apprentice, aren't you? I heard you've been running around town, helping people out. You're such a good person."

"Y-yeah… Where did you hear that from?"

"Here and there. At the market and on the street. I've heard about it from a few people."

"Wow… I wonder why." I sat up. "Do you think it's because of the magic parade Sophie and I held? Maybe everyone saw me helping her."

"What magic parade?"

"You know, the one during the Celebration of Worlds."

"Ah… Those were some fireworks. I heard one of the Seven Sages came to help Lady Faust. Our Lady Faust must be quite the historic figure."

"Yeah… Erm, did you know about me?"

"No, I'm sorry. I didn't realize you were part of the parade. It was so crowded that I doubt many people had the chance to see you. You know how packed with tourists Lapis gets during the festival."

"That's true…"

I was under the impression that I'd become famous thanks to

my role working with a world-renowned witch, but it was likely that the townspeople didn't even know I'd been part of the parade at all.

All I did during the festival was help Sophie. Anyone there to see the show was there to see her. Just how it was uncommon to know the faces and names of staff at an event, or the manager of a celebrity, no one probably even realized I was a part of the parade at all.

The reason people around town knew me was because of the work I'd done.

I must've been working harder than I thought. It made sense, too, seeing as my life was on the line.

As I was lost in my own thoughts, the old woman brought me back to the moment by saying, "Isn't it beautiful?"

I looked up and saw what she was referring to.

From this spot, we could see the entire town of Lapis glowing under the evening sun.

This was the town I loved, and my home.

Oh, right.

It dawned upon me.

I've always loved the people who live in this town. I helped them because I wanted to.

Somewhere along the way, I'd forgotten this.

"It's your reward."

"A reward?"

"A thanks, from Lapis to its citizen who goes out of her way, every day, to make the town better—to Lapis's Witch."

"You might be right..."

* * *

I walked the grandma to her house before heading back to the station. I took the long way back.

"I'm Lapis's Witch..."

It was the nickname the granny gave me. Something about it made me proud.

My feet, which had felt like weights before, felt lighter—it made me want to skip.

I skipped through town, past the residential area, and through a crowd of people.

"Oh, it's Meg."

"Good day, Miss Witch. Are you on your way home?"

"Thanks for everything, Meg."

"There she is again! It's Meg!"

"Meeeg! Bye-byyye!"

The townspeople called out to me as I went by, and I could see their faces now.

They were the townspeople I loved. I hadn't been paying attention to them these past few days.

I thought I didn't know them, but now that I took them in, I realized I was friends with almost every one of them.

"Miss Witch."

I heard a voice call to me from behind, and I turned to see a young man wearing a suit. I knew exactly who he was.

"Oh, hey. What a coincidence. I hope you're feeling better about your job."

"Are you on your way home?"

"Nah, I'm taking a walk."

"Oh, perfect. I have something for you to thank you for the other day."

He took out a paper bag, and I took it, saying, "Thanks." It had freshly baked bread in it.

"Wow, this is from that bakery on the corner. This is my teacher's favorite."

"I actually just bought it. I was going to go bring it to you."

"That would be a trip. You didn't need to do that."

The man shook his head.

"I wanted to thank you. It felt like my head was about to explode the other day with how stressful my work was, but I had no one to talk to about it. When you showed up out of nowhere and listened to me…it honestly felt like you saved me."

"That's a bit dramatic."

"I still remember what you told me."

"Did I say something good?"

"You told me I should be proud of myself."

"Oh?"

"Yeah, you said I should always be proud of myself. That sometimes things might not work out, but I should always believe in myself, no matter what. Your words really stuck with me."

After he said this, he bowed respectfully.

"When you found me, nothing I tried was going right, and… well, it made me lose confidence in myself. But you let me know that if I was doing what I was supposed to be doing, then everything was all right. Your words really pulled me out of a dark place."

"Hey, c'mon. All I did was lend an ear. You don't have to bow like that."

"Oh, I…"

"The bread is more than enough. If you ever have any more trouble, I'm always willing to lend a hand. Or an ear."

The man looked up and quietly smiled.

"Okay. I might take you up on that offer. It's good to know that Lapis's Witch is on my side."

* * *

I watched him go and took a deep breath.

"Lapis's Witch. That's a fine witch name, is it not, Meg?"

I turned around and found the Eternal Witch, Lady Faust, standing behind me.

"Oh, Teacher. What are you doing here?"

"I came to get you—my silly apprentice who left the house to walk around town without cleaning or getting dinner ready."

"Oof," I grunted, but there was something else on my mind.

"Did you say 'witch name'?"

For a witch to have a name was a great honor and a sign that she had accomplished something great.

My teacher nodded and said, "I did. Witch names are treated like a badge of honor these days, but they are actually something witches receive from the people."

"From the people..."

"When they accept you as their witch, they give you a special name that carries their thanks and trust. This is where witch names come from, and the people now call you Lapis's Witch." My teacher continued with her trademark slight smile on her face. "You are Lapis's Witch, Meg Raspberry."

"Me? I'm Lapis's Witch?"

"To those people, Meg, you are no longer Lady Faust's apprentice but Meg Raspberry, the witch."

"Oh..."

When my teacher said this, I picked up on something about the day.

Before today, everyone around town called me Lady Faust's apprentice.

But now they all knew my name and called me by it.

"No one recognizes you as a witch."

"Why do you study magic?"

"You are studying magic without a clear reason to do so. This is the reason no one recognizes you as a witch, despite learning under Faust."

I remembered what Sophie had said to me the day I met her, and felt like I finally understood what she meant.

I'd studied magic without having a real reason to. I didn't have any goal or purpose; I simply did because I thought I was supposed to.

But ever since I started collecting tears of joy, I had an actual reason to learn magic. I was learning magic to help people—to make them happy.

Seeing me do this was what made the townspeople accept me as their witch.

I could feel my chest tighten and my eyes getting warm, and I bit my lip.

Seeing me do this, my teacher gave me a satisfied smile before taking a few steps. "Let us return home, Meg. It's cold tonight. I feel like stew."

"Wait, really?! You haven't made stew in so long! What's the special occasion?"

"What do you mean? You've just received your witch name. That's definitely a cause for celebration."

"Teacher…" I sniffled. "Oh, I almost forgot. I have some fresh bread. It's your favorite!"

"Well, we'd better get home before it cools, I suppose."

"Aw yeah, I'm gonna eat till I explode!"

I ran up and walked alongside my teacher. We could smell the fresh bread as the setting sun beautifully illuminated the evening sky.

"Hey, Teacher."

"Yes?"

"I know what you meant earlier about not using magic at all today."

I looked up at my teacher as I said this.

"You said it would ruin me, not because I couldn't use the shards of emotion I gained with it but because of my magic."

My teacher met my gaze straightaway with stern eyes, and I continued.

"I used to think that learning more and getting better at magic would be enough, but I was wrong."

She remained silent, listening to me speak.

"It's strange. The power of magic you use to help others is far more powerful than I thought." Magic that brought smiles to peoples' faces. The same people who shed tears of joy, all for me. "I realized that magic isn't about skill or knowledge, but how much your heart is in it."

This was something the witches and wizards of ancient times knew, and it was the most important part of magic—of being a witch.

"Meg. The journey to become a great witch starts from that sole realization."

"Yeah?"

"There are mages who perish before they ever realize this, but you have."

"Do you think I'll ever become a great witch like you?"

"That, my dear, depends on you."

Then it dawned on me to ask something I had been thinking about for quite a while.

"Is this something to do with the reason you took me in as an apprentice...?"

The Eternal Witch, Faust, showed a somewhat happy grin before answering.

"Who knows?"

She then looked away.

I guess I'm not getting an answer today, either.

We could hear the laughter of playing children mixed in with a car puttering by as the town's sky turned crimson.

It was a busy night, and its people seemed a bit tired on their way home after a long day of work.

I loved this town.

As I helped more and more people, I learned how to handle a variety of problems. This slowly turned into a question of efficiency, with my first full tears of joy being the fuel for my efforts. This made me lose sight of what was most important: the feelings of those I was helping.

Thinking about what the person needed, sometimes learning something new to help, and giving it everything I had.

This was the reason I had grown—because I was doing my best for others. It was something I could be proud of, and it gave the tears of joy more value than just as a tool to extend my life.

These tears bound me to people who gave so much more back to me. They represented my relationships with people, lessons learned, experiences shared, and they were a part of my heart... Each and every one was a gift from the people I loved most. It was most evident when I strolled through town, as everyone who approached me was someone I'd helped.

As my teacher and I walked home together, White-Owl appeared from nowhere to perch on my arm.

"Ah! There you are! Where were you hiding?"

"Hoot."

My aloof familiar was quite the rascal, but I loved him either way.

I'll let it slide today.

"Come, Meg. We must return home before the stew gets cold."

"Oh, right! Here I come!"

I was able to learn a bit more about what was most important to a witch.

I knew there was still a lot I didn't know, but I also knew everything I'd done until now was not for nothing.

Tied to my belt was a bottle full of tears of joy. Each of the glimmering tears inside this bottle was like a medal to me, my treasure.

I had only ten months left to live, and I was living my life in a way I would never forget.

I looked at my two faithful familiars and quietly chuckled.

"Let's go home."

Epilogue:
The
Lonely
Witch

A train stopped at the station in the town of Lapis, and when its doors opened, a single old woman peered out.

Her name was Faust, and she was one of the top three witches in the world.

Everyone in town knew she was a great witch. They respected and revered her.

"Oh dear, my shoulders ache from today's travels."

Her shoulder cracked loudly as she moved it gingerly. Though she could stop herself from aging further, she couldn't hide her age.

She had been off performing her Sage duties for a long time, and her house had been empty while she was gone. Though magic kept the house dust-free, she never liked leaving her house vacant for too long. She enjoyed living alone, but it was inconvenient that there was no one to watch her home while she was away.

Faust walked out of the station and through the town. There was no need to walk, really—magic could take her where she needed to go, after all—but she wanted to look around. Taking in the town every now and then was important to her.

As she walked through the streets, many people saw her, but no one approached. They all watched in silence as she went by. Faust could tell they were distancing themselves from her, not to open up a path for her but out of awe and fear. Faust, the great witch, was unapproachable.

"Their stares always make these walks uncomfortable."

Sighing to herself, she continued down the street.

This was when a young child ran and overtook her from behind. He had to jump out of the way to avoid her, but in doing so, he fell over and twisted his ankle.

"Are you all right?"

Faust squatted down and offered the child a hand, but then…

"Boy! What do you think you're doing?! I'm so sorry, Lady Faust! Children can be so clumsy and rude!"

…a woman appeared and groveled on the ground in front of Faust.

"Ah, it's quite all right. No one was harmed, and that's what…"

Before Faust could finish, the mother got up, grabbed her kid, and ran away, leaving behind a crowd of people who saw only Faust standing there.

"My, what a ruckus."

Faust stood slowly, looking forward once again, and all gazes averted from her.

She then continued her walk home with a hint of gloom in her expression.

By the time she got home, it was completely dark outside. The only thing there to greet her was the manor itself.

"I'm home."

She called out, though there was no one to answer. Just a dark, quiet home.

"Maybe I should prepare dinner…"

Faust ate alone, with nothing but the clinking of her knife and fork on the plate and the ticking clock on the wall to keep her company.

As she enjoyed her stew, a dish she made often, she thought to herself.

When was it that I set out to become a great witch?

It was a long, long time ago. I believe it started when the witch who became my teacher paid me a compliment.

"Faust. You will become a great witch one day, I know it. I want you to become a witch who helps others, who makes people happy. A witch who is a friend to the people, who makes them smile..."

Though her memory was becoming clouded, she still remembered her teacher's words clearly. She recalled feeling happy about the recognition and how infatuated she got with learning all she could about magic.

How much time has passed since then? Since I've become a great witch recognized by all? The people depend on me, and I've helped them. I honed my skills and learned all I could, building up the experience I needed. But no one smiles when they see me. They look at me like that mother from earlier did—with fear.

When...did I become a witch everyone fears so much?

"It appears I've lost my appetite..."

The plate full of stew had gone completely cold.

It was chance that brought Faust and the girl together.

The Council of Magic had taken in a young girl, and Faust saw a light deep within her eyes. She could tell the young girl had hope—the sort of hope that could bring people together.

"Come. From today, we are family, Meg Raspberry."

Over ten years had passed since that day.

A train stopped at the station in the town of Lapis, and when its doors opened, a single old woman peered out.

She was one of the top three witches in the world.

"My, I'm having to leave town more and more these days."

It was a long trip, but the woman had nothing to worry about—save for the off chance that her apprentice was up to her antics.

Tired from the journey, the woman thought about how she might have her apprentice massage her shoulders when she got home.

"Welcome back, Lady Faust."

As soon as she stepped through the gate, a man who worked at the train station approached her.

"I saw Meg today. She was being chased by a stampede of animals."

"What did she do this time…?"

Evidently, antics *were* on the schedule that day. Faust's apprentice always found a way to get into trouble when she wasn't around. It kept her young, though.

Faust walked out of the station and through the town. There was no need to walk, really—magic could take her where she needed to go, after all—but she wanted to look around. Taking in the town every now and then was important to her.

As she walked through the streets, people who passed her acknowledged her with respectful nods.

"Welcome home, Lady Faust."

"Meg was at the market today. She bought a boatload of groceries. She said there was going to be a feast tonight."

"Thank you for the other day. How's Meg?"

"Lady Faust, you need to teach young Meg some manners. She keeps trying to haggle me out of my bread."

People were approaching Faust much more in recent years.

They all talked about Meg, letting the woman know whenever they saw her larger-than-life apprentice running around town.

Faust thought about how Meg connected her to this town and its people.

As she thought this, she noticed a young girl fall over up ahead. It looked like she'd hurt her foot.

"Are you all right, young one?"

Faust approached the young girl carefully. She helped the child up, and it looked like the girl was uninjured.

"Lady Faust! Thank you!"

She knew this girl, and her identity became evident when a man came running up to the two.

"Oh, Lady Faust. Thank you."

"Hendy. Is this your daughter?"

"Yes. Her name is Anna. Are you all right, Anna?"

"I'm fine! Hey, Lady Faust. How's Meg?"

"She's doing well. Almost too well… She's become quite the celebrity around here. To think a girl as young as yourself would know her."

"She really helped us the other day, after all."

"Yeah! She showed us the bestest flowers in the whole wide world!"

"Is that right…?"

Faust saw Dr. Hendy and Anna off and breathed deeply while she took the town in. She felt like the town was beginning to change. The fearful looks had turned into smiling faces.

It's all thanks to her. Like the wind, little by little, Meg breathes new life into this town wherever she goes.

That wind was blowing on Faust now. The road home that was once a difficult trip for Faust was becoming easier every day.

Before long, the sun was setting. Faust could see her home as she made her way through the forest. There was a warm light coming from within, waiting to welcome her home.

She opened her front door, and sure enough, there was Meg, cooking food in a large pot and surrounded by animals, there to greet her.

"Welcome back, Teacher! You're late! I made soup for dinner tonight! You're gonna love it! Hey! C'mon, guys, give me some space! I'm cookin' here!"

Meg and the many familiars were there to greet her.

The home had cheerful voices and warm light coming from it… It had family. This sight alone brought joy to Faust's heart.

"Yes, I'm home."

Faust smiled softly.

I bet she doesn't know yet—that she will someday take on the name of Eternal Witch.

I don't have much time left.

If what I saw that day is the truth, then I have very little life remaining.

Faust was the only one aware of the truth, at this point.

But that is a story for another day.

Afterword

I extend my heartfelt gratitude to everyone who read *Once Upon a Witch's Death*. Writing novels has been a passion of mine for seventeen years, and I'm still amazed by this opportunity. Life is full of unexpected journeys, it seems.

This book's creation involved the collaboration of many incredible individuals. I owe a tremendous debt of gratitude to Chorefuji, my talented illustrator, and to Tabata, my dedicated editor. Words cannot fully express my deep appreciation for your invaluable support.

Most importantly, I wish to thank each of you who took the time to delve into my story. Among the myriad of books available, the fact that you chose and read mine is a gift I cherish deeply. My sincerest thanks to you all.

Meg's journey unveiled countless dreams to me, and it is my hope that her story inspires you to chase what is important to you as well.

Saka